Just So Christmas Stories

Tony Hoffmann

This is a work of fiction. Names, characters, places, and incidents are the products of the author's imagination. If a situation appears to be real it is used fictitiously.

Copyright 2018 Tony Hoffmann

TonyHoffmannBooks.com

Cover design and layout by Andrew Knaupp

Third U.S. Edition 2018
Second U.S. Edition 2012
(First Edition was named "Five Treasured Christmas Stories." This edition includes the original five stories from the first edition and eight additional stories.)

A note from the author

Just So Christmas Stories is a collection of thirteen short stories describing the lives of 13 different people in unique circumstances who found the spirit of Christmas in their own way.

It is a reflection of different people who interact with each other and their surroundings. You may identify yourself with any one of the characters or relate to their situation(s). There is a little bit of everyone in this collection.

We hope through the sadness, sorrows, and happiness in the stories you will find the hope, and joy of what Christmas is about, a celebration of the life that Jesus Christ led. Yes it is about his divine birth, the fulfillment of ancient prophecies, the wise men, shepherds abiding their flocks in the fields, angels announcing his birth, and the star in the east.

However, it is more than that, it is about his ministry. Christmas is about Jesus having compassion on the woman taken in adultery, giving sight to the blind man, healing the leper, comforting the widow of Nain, raising Lazarus from the dead. It is a celebration of loving one another and serving one another as a manifestation of that love.

These stories incorporate acts of kindness, compassion, healing, and hope. My hope, as you read them, is that your tears will fall and through those tears you will feel uplifted. And most of all, I hope you will give of yourself to some one else. In the poem The Vision of Sir Launfal, by James Russell Lowell, Sir Launfal, after his failed quest for the holy grail, was told by the leper who he shares his last moldy crust of bread with, who then appears to him "…glorified, shining and tall and fair and straight," tells him, "not what we give, but what we share– For the gift without the giver is bare; Who gives himself with his alms feeds three, – Himself, his hungering neighbor, and Me."

May this Christmas season change your heart. May all the Christmasses thereafter change the hearts of others you have served.

Enjoy the Just So Christmas Stories. Grab a rich cup of hot chocolate, a warm blanket, and snuggle up on the couch surrounded by your family and read the Just So Christmas Stories by the light of the crackling fire.

Merry Christmas.

Tony Hoffmann

Contents

The Magic Clock

Wesley Beacham lay on his bed staring out the frost covered window watching the snowflakes fall from the sky as they effortlessly floated toward earth. The luminescence of the full moon made the myriad of flakes easier to see as they journey downward from the pull of gravity. Christmas was in a couple of days. Just the excitement of anticipating the day caused sleep to evade Wesley's eyes.

Christmas had always been a magical time in the Beacham house. Traditions ran deep, holiday cheer abounded, and festivities were fanciful and fun. The entire month of December was a magical month of memories. This Christmas was spent at his grandfather's home in a quiet little cottage, in a quiet little town, forgotten by time.

Wesley was laying on a large, four-poster, wooden feather bed, covered with a large feather filled comforter, surrounded by large feather pillows. He was tucked into the featheriness like a gosling, tucked under mother gooses wing, snug and warm. It was especially cozy since the old house had no furnace except for a large, single, potbelly wood stove that sat in a stone fireplace in the family room. It kept most of the house toasty except for the outer extremities, like a couple bedrooms and the bathroom, which made it the place to avoid at night.

Wesley's grandfather's grandfather had built the house. He raised his family there, as did his son, and his son's son. The home itself was a tradition. Every third or fourth year the family would all gather together in this old home which had been added onto numerous times, and had been renovated several more. It was funny that in all that adding and renovating no one ever thought to put in a furnace. But for some reason the old stove somehow seemed to keep up with Father Winter and had the uncanny ability to chase away Jack Frost and keep its occupants toasty warm. And where it fell short, the goose down comforters and accouterments seemed to pick up the slack.

Staring out the moonlit window on that night Wesley was visualizing the horse drawn sleighs the family would ride on Christmas Eve down snow covered Kensington Lane then across Middleton Meadow and on

1

to Pendleton's pond. During the summer Pendleton's Pond was a favorite fishing and swimming hole for all the young boys of the village because it was always crystal clear and clean. Aspen trees and tall evergreen trees dotted the landscape around the pond with tall green grass, interlaced with little blue, yellow, and violet flowers made it a favorite picnic spot for families on Sunday.

When winter came, and the snow fell, the landscape took on a majestic, crisp appearance. The pond now appeared a crystal clear deep blue, the grand fir trees had boughs of snow on their branches, and the aspens where ghostly figures against the moonlight.

This enchanted sleigh ride happen every Christmas Eve. The horses were harnessed to the sleighs, warm blankets would be draped around the riders, gloves with knitted hats and wool mufflers would guard against the cold and chilly air as it would try and nip at their cheeks as the horses trotted down the path toward the pond.

When they arrived they would all step down from the sleigh, gather around a large rectangular stone table, and drape the blankets around their shoulders instead of over their laps. They would watch as grandfather began the candle lighting ceremony. He would stand at the opposite side of the stone table upon which were seven white candles, in seven golden candlesticks, and in front of each of the candlesticks would be a sprig of green holy with three red berries. He would retrieve a very long match and strike it against the box. As the flame of the match burst into existence he would touch each of the wicks of the candles with the flame and explain what each candle with the holly represented.

Once all the candles were lit they would stand around the table holding hands and sing Christmas carols. The harmonic sound would echo out over the pond and into the dark woods. Wesley could just imagine the woodland ferries sitting on mistletoe leaves with fluttering wings as they listened to the enchanted music as it reverberated in and among the trees.

Just as the carols would conclude, hot wassail and gingerbread cookies seemed to somehow appear out of nowhere on the stone table. Steam would rise from the cups and ginger would fill the air. Oh how good it would feel to cradle that cup of hot wassail in your fingers. As they stood sipping on the wassail and munching on gingerbread cookies grandpa would begin the story of the magical clock.

"The village clock maker built a magical clock many hundreds of years ago in this very village on a Christmas Eve. It wasn't just any clock, nor just any magical clock, but a very special magical clock. He didn't build it with the intent to make it a magical clock, but that is what happened.

The wood of this clock was said to have come from an old monastery that used to be just over the hills to the east. The monk's of the monastery claimed the wood came from the same wood used to build the manger the Christ child was laid in on the first Christmas day. The story was told of how the clock maker was given the wood when the old monastery was destroyed by fire and the only thing left was the wood of the manger.

The village clock maker would spend every evening after his regular work to cut, glue, and fit together the wood of the old clock. He would sand and sand the old wood until it was as smooth as glass. Then the clock maker would search and search all the surrounding villages and hamlets to find springs and gears and cogs and wheels and jewels from other old clocks, some from far away lands and different times, and then piece them all together with precision in order to form the intricate timing mechanisms of the magical clock.

The pieces used in this magical clock were said to have come from the timepieces of the Sultans of Arabia, the Knights of the Crusades, the Emperors of Asia, and the Kings of Europe. Each piece had traveled long distances and had been handed down from one keeper to another until they had become lost or abandoned and wound up in a tinkers shop broken down waiting for the right clock maker to see its disguised value and resurrect and unite each piece into a new time and a new purpose.

And so it was that this village clock maker had gathered all of the mechanism necessary to create a magnificent clock. The wood for the clock was from old olive wood, the two hands of the clock were made of gold, the face of the clock was from pearl, the roman numerals from one to twelve were of silver, and the gears, cogs, springs, and wheels of the finest brass. Carved into the wood of the clock were the seven symbols of Christmas, the star, a lighted candle, a holly leaf, a dove, a snowflake, a bell, and an angel.

When the clock maker had finally finished his clock he gently inserted the winding key into the slot on the back of the clock and turned the key seven times until the main spring was wound tight. He removed the key and slid it into the ivory holder on the back of the clock. The clockmaker bent his ear close to the pearl face of the clock and listened to the mesmerizing sound of the ticking and the toking of the fine brass parts as they synchronized together to track time.

The story is told of how the clockmaker set the clock on his wooden mantel after he had finished the making of the clock. After touching the fine wood finish he bent over and lit a fire in the stone hearth.

Turning towards his bed he removed the slippers from his feet and the nightcap from his head, and knelt down by his old wood and rope bed. He said a prayer expressing his gratitude for finishing the clock and for the divine help he felt he received in piecing it all together in such a fine and detailed manner. After his sincere prayer was over he slipped between his straw filled mattress and his down comforter and fell fast asleep resting his head on his big feather pillows.

Once the clockmaker's eyes were closed and the soft but steady breathing of his sleep filled the air, the room began to fill with light. A slight warm breeze blew the curtains of his window from side to side and the gentle shuffling of soft feet could be heard on the wooden floor of his cottage. An angel in a flowing white robe could have been seen to move towards the clock on the mantel if eyes had been awake to see her come in. She stood in front of the flickering fire, robes rippling, and long white hair shimmering down her back. She admired the handiwork of the clock. She looked at every detail of the clock, the golden hands, the silver numbers, the beautiful olive wood, and the symbols carved into the case. She even leaned her head towards the ticking of the clock so her ears could listen to the almost melodic sound it gave off.

It is said the angel reached out her finger and touched the pearl face

4

of the clock as it marked the time as 2:22 am. A bright glow emanated from the center of the clock and streaks of white light darted and flickered all around the clock almost as if it were a mini fireworks show of the brightest white light. When the dancing of the lights had ceased the angel in the white flowing robes and the long white shimmering hair turned and walked toward the clockmaker sleeping on the bed. Stopping at the side of his bed she looked at his kind, gentle face and touched his cheek with her finger causing the skin on his face to glow. A smile crept onto the clockmaker's face as if his dreams had suddenly been filled with joy. The curtains of the window blew, a light flashed out, and all was dark except the glowing coals of the fire below the clock.

It was said that now every 25th of December, at 2:22 am the person who winds the clock would be given a magical wish of time. The story would conclude with the sad ending that many years later the clock disappeared during a fire that raged throughout the village. The cottage of the clockmaker of this provincial little town was burned and destroyed. When the fire brigades and rescuers came into the village, most of the village was burned to the ground, except for a stone fireplace and a wooden mantel, which didn't have so much as a single burn mark on it. However, no clock was to be found."

After the telling of the story everyone would sigh and wonder what ever happened to the magical clock? Was the story even true? Slowly the family would make their way to the edge of the water of Pendleton's Pond where a wooden beam supported by two vertical wooden posts held 7 bells hanging from seven red ribbons. Each bell was a different size and each bell would be rung seven times ringing out the notes of a special song only the Beacham's knew. Once the song of the bells had been played a cage with seven white doves in it would be opened and the doves released. They would rush into the air and fly free from the cage. Wesley loved to see the doves' wings flutter, as they flew towards the silvery moon across the calm reflective waters of Pendleton's pond.

The sleigh ride back to the old house would be filled with excitement and anticipation of presents to be opened, songs to be sung, food to be eaten, and laughter to be heard, and family to be hugged. What wonderful memories would be made. Wesley rolled on his side in the big feather bed and hoped that this Christmas Eve would hold the same magic all the others had held. His eyes were now getting heavy, his body relaxed, and the warmth and comfort of the bed caused sleep to settle on his mind.

The next morning Wesley rose from the warmth of his comforter to the frigid air of the bedroom. He felt he couldn't get his cloths on fast enough. Once the task had been accomplished he'd race through the house to the stone fireplace wherein sat the potbelly stove, with a fine wooden mantel above it. It had been loaded with wood again in the early hours of the morning by his grandpa Joe.

Today, the Eve of Christmas Eve, was the traditional day that the men of the family would all brave the cold of the East Mountain to find the perfect Christmas tree that would grace the living room of the Beacham's cottage. It couldn't just be any tree. It had to be a Balsam Fir, thin at the top, full at the bottom, perfectly tapered and resplendent with fragrance. It had to be just large enough so the star on top could almost touch the ceiling and just round enough to fit in the corner of the family room and hold all of the special ornaments and lights.

The women and girls in the family would then bake the most mouth watering, soft sugar cookies that should only have been possible in dreams. The air would be filled with the aroma of the baking cookies and the counters would be filled with the cooling of those already baked. It was a wonderful arrangement between the moms and dads and brothers and sisters of the Beacham clan.

Mid afternoon the bedraggled men would clomp into the cottage with the prized tree and the whooping and hollering of all would fill the air as they nailed on the wooden stand and set the tree upright making sure it was perfectly vertical and that the best side was showing. The smell of the sugar cookies and the Balsam Fir would mixed together to enliven the senses of all, and remind them that Christmas Eve was just around the corner.

As the winter sun was beginning to set in the western sky that evening, and the temperatures began to drop, Wesley sat on the old wooden steps in front of the wrap around porch, his hands holding up his chin. He stared into the large orange sun as it was sneaking below the snow-covered horizon getting ready for morning on the other side of the world. His thoughts were taking him back to grandpa's story of the legend of the magical clock. Questions began to fill his mind such as; did the magical clock really exist, what had happened to the clock maker, if the fireplace, where the clock maker had set the clock, was still intact, where had the clock gone? Did someone take it? If it were really magical, did it just hide itself from the flames or disappear to a magical land? So many questions he thought, but no answers, and nowhere to find them.

His mind meandered onto the magical wish of time to the one who winds the clock at 2:22 am. What exactly did the wish of time mean? Was it like the three wishes granted to the person who found Aladdin's lamp and rubbed it? Could a person actually wish for more wishes? He then thought about time. It wasn't something he really thought about much, well, actually, he never thought of time, at least not as an object or possession. He was too young to worry about time, especially time flying as his grandparents would say, or now as his father started to say. How did time fly anyways?

Whatever the wish of time was, all he knew was that if he found the clock, he would have a wish. To him, it seemed a very serious thing to think about, especially if all you got was one wish. It would have to be something thought out and planned well before the moment came for requesting the wish. But before he got too far ahead of himself with the wish stuff, he needed to figure out where this magical clock could be found; after all, tomorrow was Christmas Eve.

Wesley said goodnight to his mom and dad, his grandparents, and the other family members that had congregated at grandpas house. He climbed into his warm flannel pajamas and pulled the thick down comforter up to his chin. His little mind darted from one Christmas thought to the next until sleep overtook his eyes and once again he lay motionless in his feathery goodness.

Today was the day…it was Christmas Eve. The Beacham's tradition each year for Christmas Eve day was for everyone, grown ups and children alike, to make decorations. The kitchen table was filled with colored paper, strings, ribbons, scissors, glue, popsicle sticks, yarn, glitter, crayons, toothpicks, and cotton balls. All that was required was imagination, fun, and a great attitude. Strings of stars and snowflakes would be made and hung on the walls, origami Santa's and reindeer would ornament the coffee table, popsicle Christmas trees with crayon lights would hang from the door lintels, toothpick manger scenes with paper camels would sit on the end tables, and yarn and glitter glued to paper that would spell out Merry Christmas would be hung above the tree.

The day was filled with fun, family and anticipation. It was probably the longest day of the year for Wesley, other than his birthday. For some reason he thought, the day always seemed to get longer when presents were involved. But as days do, the minutes and the hours tick away and before everyone knows it, the time for celebration is here.

Just as Wesley had envisioned it two days before, when he was all snuggled between the comforter and pillows of his bed, so the evening went. The sleigh rides in the snow, the lighting of the candles, the singing of the songs, the drinking of the wassail, the telling of the legend of the magical clock, the ringing of the bells, and the freeing of the doves. It was all just as wonderful if not more wonderful than it had been the last time they were at grandpa Joe's cottage. In fact, Wesley had enjoyed it so much more as he was now a little older than the last time they were there.

As the horse drawn sleighs pulled into the barn Wesley could feel the snowflakes melt on his face. His cheeks were rosy, his clothes moist with sweat, and his heart happy. He raced into the house with the rest of the family as grandpa wiped down the horses and put away the sleighs.

As the family gathered together in the living room of the cottage Wesley found himself in grandpa's recliner staring at the beautiful Christmas tree. His little heart felt as if it were about to burst with the joy. He carefully studied each of the ornaments on the tree, the toy nutcracker, the pink ballerina, the little red caboose, the red and white striped candy canes, the silver bells, the winged angels, and the shiny stars. Each one added its own special goodness to the Balsam Fir. Christmas was such a magical time of year, especially for little boys and little girls.

Grandpa had finally come in and lifted Wesley onto his lap as he sat down in his favorite recliner. Wesley leaned his head onto grandpa Joe's chest. The evening celebrations began with a prayer of gratitude offered for the baby Jesus. Then songs of Christmas were sung, stories were read, instruments were played, the nativity scene acted out, and finally gifts were exchanged. Time seemed to stop in Wesley's mind. Everything seemed to move in slow motion, the laughter, the hugging, the conversing, the eating, the gift wrappings piling up on the floor, all of it seemed surreal and amazing to the eyes of Wesley as he watched Christmas happen before his eyes. He had no words to describe how he felt; he only knew it felt good.

Before he knew it, he and the rest of the children were hustled off to bed where they would try and sleep waiting for Santa to come and fill the stockings that were hanging by the fireplace with care. As he did every year he would try to stay awake so he could see the jolly white bearded man in red. And just as would happen every year he would not realize that he had fallen asleep.

Wesley wasn't sure how long he had been asleep, or what time it was, or if he was awake or asleep, all he was aware of was the steady ticking of a sound. Everything seemed quiet and still, all except the ticking that seemed to be going off in his head.

He was convinced somewhere in the tangled reality of his sleeping mind that the ticking was just that, a part of his dreams. He turned onto his side, then his back, then his side again, thinking he needed to make himself more comfortable, yet all the while this ticking sound kept going off in his brain. It seemed to get louder and louder until he finally decided he needed to wake up to make it all go away.

His eyes opened to a dark room filled with the faint light of the moon. He stared out the window again and saw that more snow was falling. As he was coming into consciousness he was aware that the ticking sound hadn't gone away when he woke up. It was still there, the steady, rhythmic tick-tock, tick-tock, tick-tock. It was the sound of a clock. He sat up in his bed and adjusted his head so as to allow his ears to more fully differentiate where the sound was coming from. It most definitely was a clock. He threw back the covers of his bed and slipped his little feet into his warm slippers and put on his thick robe. He walked past the other children in the room and out into the hallway listening to the sound of the clock. He walked slowly down the hallway all the while listening to the sound that to him seemed to echo throughout the entire house. He was now in the family room where some of the gown ups were sleeping on the floor.

"Strange," he thought to himself, "no one seemed to hear or notice the ticking and the tocking of the clock." To him it was a loud and steady tick-tock, tick-tock, tick-tock. Quietly he walked through the house trying to follow the steady sound of the clock. Softly he opened up the bedroom doors and peered in intently listening for the sound of the tick-tock. When he was certain it was not coming from that room he walked to the next and the next until he was out of bedrooms.

Tiptoeing he went into the bathroom, then the kitchen, then the pantry, and then into the old creepy water heater room. Nothing. He then tiptoed to his grandpa's office and quietly opened the door. There was grandpa sitting at his desk, asleep, holding what looked like a small wooden statue of a horse. He glanced around the room and decided the sound was not coming from grandpa's office either. In fact, the sound didn't come from any of the rooms in the house, yet there it was, as a steady drum beat in a quiet jungle. There were only two places left, and both of them scared Wesley. One was the cellar below the house, and the other was the attic above the house.

At this point Wesley began to think that the ticking sound must be coming from inside his head and not from the house as no one else was awake wondering what that tick-tock sound was? He was determined at that point to climb back into his warm feather bed and sleep the sound away. Yet another part of his mind wouldn't let him leave it alone. But the cellar was even creepier than the water heater room and it had cobwebs, mice pooh, and dead bugs on the floor!

Yet he decided he needed to override his fears and look in the cellar. He turned the old knob of the old door that led into the old stairway that led down into the old cellar. On the old shelf just inside the old stairway was an old metal flashlight. Wesley grabbed the light and clicked the switch on. A yellow dim beam of light shown out in a circle and he could see the dusty steps leading downward. He gulped and took his first step, then the next and the next and the next and creek went the wood of the step causing him to stop and look back up the stairway toward the door. It wasn't too late to turn back he thought, but there was that tick-tock, tick-tock of the clock.

After several more agonizing steps he landed on the dirt floor of the cellar. Luckily for him the cellar was very small so it wouldn't take too much time to look around. It was lined with old wooden shelves that contained hundreds of Kerr jars filled with strange looking things that must have been food of some kind. Upon closer inspection he saw that they were green beans, squash, peaches, and other fruits and vegetables. He wasn't sure though that he wanted to eat these things as they looked like they belonged in Frankenstein's laboratory.

He shone the light around but couldn't see anything. Plus he realized the sound had become quieter. The origination of the noise definitely didn't come from here. "I'm done," he said, and just as quickly he ran to the stairs and up them, two steps at a time, breathing a sigh of relief when he finally reached the door. He couldn't turn off the flashlight and shut to the door fast enough. Goose bumps ran the whole length of his arms and neck.

"Okay," he thought, "then the sound must be coming from the attic." This was not as creepy as the cellar at night, but still would require a certain amount of courage as it was still filled with cobwebs and boxes. But there were two windows, one at each end of the attic, and there was a full moon, so there should be enough light to make him feel less anxiety.

Within moments he was climbing the narrow thin steps up to the attic. As he approached the top of the stairs a bluish light shone through the window and illuminated the attic in muted light and shadow. He looked around at all the different things that were stored up here. The sound he realized was louder here than downstairs in the main part of the house. In fact it seemed clearer, more precise, almost as if it was beckoning him to come closer and see.

Wesley walked softly and quietly across the dusty wooden floor towards the sound. When he was about half way to the other side he noticed the spaces between the dusty wooden slats on the floor were glowing. Beams of light were shining up through the wood and getting tangled in the swirling dust his feet had made. He stopped and knelt down by the light. The sound of the clock was the loudest here. He bent his head towards the floor putting his ears to the wood. There it was, the rhythmic steady sound of tick-tock, tick-tock, tick-tock.

He put his small fingers into a knothole he saw in the wood in the floor and pulled up with his finger. To his surprise the wood lifted easily. In fact, it lifted in a square with other wood slats all stuck together at the same time. It was a small trap door. He bent the trap door over and laid it on the floor exposing the compartment below and gasped as the light from the compartment made his face glow. Looking into the space he saw where the sound had come from. There, lying in the compartment, was a wooden box with the symbol of a clock carved into its lid.

Wesley reached in and pulled the box out and set it on the floor next to him. There was a latch covering a clasp but there was no lock. Slowly he lifted the latch and raised the lid to the box. There inside the wooden box was a clock, a beautiful, magnificent, clock. He was astonished as he stared down at the clock. The face of the clock was white like a pearl, the minute and hour hands were made of gold, and the numbers were sliver. "This must be the magical clock," he thought to himself! "But it can't be," yet there it was, right in front of him.

He reached into the box and pulled out the clock and set it on the floor next to him. He looked on the backside of the clock and saw a key sticking out of an ivory holder. He pulled the key out and just looked at it. It was a beautiful key with ornate scrolls on the handle. On the back of the clock was a keyhole. Wesley took the key and slid it into the keyhole and turned the key. He was able to only turn it seven times. He lifted the clock and looked at the hands on the face of it and to his surprise the time read 2:22. It was now early morning on December 25th, 2:22 am.

The clock had been wound.

As Wesley Beacham held the clock the tick-tock sound suddenly stopped. The air and light in the room began to coalesce and move in large concentric patterns. Wesley looked up and became mesmerized by the sight of the swirling light and air. It moved about the room in between the cardboard boxes and around the wooden chairs and between the metal trunks, darting toward the ceiling, and then plunging to the floor coursing over the wooden planks and climbing back up the walls. It was patterns, it was shapes, it was movement, and it filled the entire room in a moving fog until the objects in the room were no longer visible.

The air felt thick yet light and airy. Wesley stood up amidst the swirl of light and air and moved his head side-to-side trying to understand what was happening. It seemed to go on for the longest time yet mere moments had past. All of sudden the thick air swirled in tighter and tighter circles moving upwards toward the ceiling like a tornado twisting around itself until it suddenly vanished! All was gone. When Wesley looked around he was no longer standing in the attic with the magic clock.

He was standing in a different version of the family room of his grandfather's house, looking at a woman lighting candles on a magnificent tree that was decked with silver tinsel, paper ornaments, popcorn on string, small pieces of fruit, colored yarn, and glass bulbs of every color. He looked about the room and saw children of all ages sitting on the floor and on the laps of older people. He saw an auburn Irish setter dog, an old man sitting in a wooden rocker and old vintage vignette photographs on the wall. The people were singing Silent Night as the candles on the tree were being lit.

Wesley's mind was confused, where was he, when was he, who were these people? He looked at each of the people trying to study their faces. For some reason they seemed familiar to him? Where had he seen them? He looked at the wall with pictures and slowly walked over to them.

Looking at the pictures on the wall he realized he had seen these pictures before. They were in his grandfather's photo album that he had seen earlier this week. He turned and looked again at all the people and recognized his grandfather in the face of the little seven-year-old boy sitting in front of the tree singing his heart out. The woman lighting the candles on the tree was his grandfather's mother and his grandfather's father was playing the squeezebox tapping his toe to the beat.

All of a sudden Wesley remembered the story his grandfather had told him the day they were cutting down the Balsam Fir on East Mountain. He had told him of his favorite Christmas when he was a boy. How much fun he had and the wonderful memories. How the whole family had gathered together in the old cottage, how his mother had made pies and cookies and decorations and how the presents under the Christmas tree seemed to fill the room. Each gift was handcrafted or made with love by each person there and how they shared those talents and gifts with each other. He spoke of the feeling, a feeling so strong you could almost cut it with a knife, the feeling of family and love, and being together on such a special day.

His grandfather remembered opening up one of his gifts and it was a horse carved out of wood. A majestic steed that was rearing up on its hind legs, head stretched high and main flowing. How he loved that present. In fact, Wesley remembered seeing it earlier this very night when he was peeking in trying to locate the sound of the ticking clock. It was sitting on his grandpa's chest as he sat sleeping in his office. His grandfather spoke of his brothers and sisters and his cousins who had all come to celebrate Christmas that year. That special Christmas still had an impact on him seventy years later.

Wesley had marveled at the story his grandfather told him as the Balsam Fir fell to the snow covered ground. He could almost feel it as he spoke the words of that Christmas day. He spoke of it with such passion and such joy just as if he were reliving it that very moment as the snow was falling and he was cutting down the Balsam Fir. As Wesley listened he felt as if he wanted to experience such a wonderful time. What would it be like to have been there? Well, as he looked around, he was there, and it was just as grandfather had told him. It was the feeling that permeated the air, the love that filled the room, the joy in everyone's faces, the happiness in their hearts, and the unity of the family bond that made this day what it was.

He watched as a gift was handed to his seven-year-old grandfather. The wrapping was torn off to reveal a magnificent stallion rearing up with a flowing main. The eyes of the seven year old were mesmerized as he held the wooden statue in his hands and fingered every detail of the carving. He held it to his chest and a single tear of happiness rolled down his face. Wesley could feel the overwhelming joy this seven-year-old boy felt sitting in that family room surrounded by love. He saw his seven-year-old grandpa give hugs to all his family and two hugs to those who had given him gifts. He then handed out his own home made gifts as well.

Grandpa had told him that one of the reasons that Christmas day held such a special feeling for him, and why he remembered it seventy years later, was that his mother would pass away only two months later of influenza. It was the last Christmas he would spend with his mother whom he loved a great deal. He would miss her greatly and every Christmas, unbeknownst to Wesley, and the other family members, he would sit in his office after the Christmas Eve celebrations were over, and everyone had gone to bed, and hold that wooden stallion to his heart and remember that wonderful Christmas.

The laughter, the chatter, the sounds of Christmas filled the air. Wesley stood by the majestic tree and was watching it all happen. As he was observing this Christmas celebration everything began to move in slow motion. The sounds began to have a distant feel to it, the scene seemed to become blurry as if it was all fading away, and the light seemed to be moving in circles. The next thing Wesley realized he was standing in the attic of grandpa Joe's house holding the magical clock.

It was still dark, the moonbeams were still shining in the windows, and he was still standing on the wooden floor with his heavy robe and fluffy slippers still on. It had been an entire evening in a moment. Was it real? He looked down at the clock and the time still read 2:22am. Time, evidently did stand still, especially for special times.

Holding on to the magical clock Wesley walked back down the stairs and into the family room. Everyone was still fast asleep. He stepped over the sleeping grown ups towards the stone fireplace. He held the clock in front of him and admired its curious workmanship. He had never seen such a beautiful clock; it must truly have been touched by an angel. He lifted the clock and rested it on the wooden mantel. When he let go of the clock it illuminated itself in little streaks of light that flurried around it in circles. The dancing lights only lasted a moment, as if to say, "I'm home," and then all went dark.

Wesley wiggled his way between the cozy feather bed and oversized comforter and stared back out the window at the full moon and more flakes of snow falling toward the ground. It truly was a magical Christmas Eve. In a few hours it would be Christmas morning and the magical clock would be a wonderful addition to the Beacham's family room. "What a gift that will be," he thought as he dosed off to sleep.

The magic clock had given Wesley a gift of time, the time to see into another's life. To not only hear, but to experience another's joy. This Christmas would be Wesley's favorite. He took that feeling with him into his life. He learned that Christmas day, that life is about others, it is about loving someone else, it was about finding joy in someone else's joys, it was about forgetting yourself and discovering someone else. Time truly is a magical gift and whom we spend that time with, makes it even more magical.

The Ring

A low muffled sound seemed to float through the darkness of the still night and enter ever so slightly into the ears of Stephen as he lay sleeping on a cold, crisp December night. His sleep of late had been sporadic at best and his dreams had been disconnected and maybe even somewhat disturbing and at this moment he had only been asleep close to three hours.

A muffled sound that seemed to come from some far away place continued to pierce his ears and gradually make its way into the consciousness of his mind until gradually he began to realize the sound was coming from next to where he had been sound asleep. Slowly the lids of his eyes opened and he found himself staring into the darkness of the night. Rolling over he searched the blackness until he found the red glow of his digital alarm clock that sat partially obscured on his nightstand, which let him know it was only 2:30 in the morning.

Stephen raised himself up on his elbow to listen more attentively in the stillness of the night to the details of the sound. Realizing the source of the muffled sound he rolled over and put his ear onto Carolyn's neck and knew that his precious wife of 25 years was crying. She had been attempting to muffle her cries so as not to wake him up. She knew he was exhausted from worry and long hours at work on top of very little sleep. Yet she welcomed his warm face against her neck and his strong arms as they reached around her.

Stephen's fingers gently felt Carolyn's face in the darkness and his rough fingers wiped the wet tears from off her cold cheeks. He let his fingers follow the trail of tears onto the pillow and found it soaked. Curled up on her side of the bed with her face buried into her pillow she had been crying in the night from the pain, the intense never ending, relentless pain. Pain, which she lacked the ability to describe, let alone endure.

She knew these were her final days. She knew her battle, which started three years ago almost to the day, was nearing its final conclusion. She had been on pain medication almost around the clock for the past week. It was the foggy reality, laced with delusional dreams and hallucinations that made her decide to reduce the amount of the medications she needed to take.

She wanted to spend her last remaining time aware of her family and the world around her and in full control of her mind. Yet the pain at times was more than she thought she could bear, and even though the tears did not alleviate the relentless pain, it was an outlet for her soul to outwardly express the inner anguish she had been called to bear.

Hope, which filled her heart on and off during the wearying treatments had faded into the distant past and was not even a memory now. Tonight, as with yesterday and the day before, she was tired, she was worn out, and she was now ready to just have it all come to the closing moments, the final curtain call.

Reality made words obsolete, Stephen could only ask so many times, "Are you all right?" Now it to came down to the unspoken language of touch and the sorrowful expression of an empathetic look. They both knew she was not all right and that she was passing through valley of the shadow of death.

Stephen gently rolled off his side of the bed and with hastened steps walked around to Carolyn's side. Bending over in a room still dark except for the ambient light that reflected off a full moon and a freshly deposited blanket of white snow Stephen's warm hand rested tenderly on the side of Carolyn's face as he bent over and kissed her forehead which was cold almost clammy. It seemed to mirror the snowy landscape just outside their frosted windowpane, the result of the recent storm that passed through earlier that evening.

Standing in their bedroom, which held a lifetime of memories, Stephen stared into Carolyn's face as his eyes finally adjusted to the available light. As her face was coming into view Stephen remembered a night long ago when he came to her side of the bed, only that time to gently, yet hurriedly help her up so she could dress while he grabbed her bags which had already been packed a couple of days earlier, anticipating this moment, and rush her in their beat up Bonneville to the maternity ward of St Mary's Hospital.

The labor had been hard and several times they thought they had lost her but after a long hard fought battle their first son was born, a healthy 7 pound 6 ounce boy with a head of hair that could have carpeted a village. Fear and worry filled Stephen's heart that night as he thought his new bride might not make it through what was suppose to be the happiest time of their lives.

Carolyn's face came into view and Stephen could see the lines of pain creased on her slender narrow face. The tears had slowed but were still ebbing out of her red and swollen eyes, as she lay curled up on the bed. The emotional pain he felt at seeing his lifelong companion suffer was an experience that tore at the very marrow of his soul. He knew this gut wrenching feeling would last a lifetime. He hugged her for a long while hoping somehow it would make it all right.

Softly Stephen pulled back the covers from off of Carolyn and folded them back on the bed. Ever so lovingly he slid his arms under her back and around her legs and lifted up his thin frail wife and cradled her into his arms. It was as if he were carrying a feather. She had never been heavy but tonight she seemed as if she weighed less than a bird with a breeze below its wings. She felt so fragile, so brittle as he held her in his arms her body curled up within his large frame.

Carolyn rested her weary head and arms against Stephens chest as he carried her down the wooden stairs while he leaned his cheek against her forehead. All the lights in the house had been turned off except the red and green lights that were emanating from the family room where the Christmas tree had been left burning. Somehow their seemed to be a magic that filled the room from those twinkling lights amid the ornaments that hung from the tinsel laden branches of the evergreen.

Entering the family room Stephen's eyes glanced at the remnants of the fire beneath the stone hearth that had now died down to only a few red coals, all that was left from the cherry wood yuletide log. He walked close to the glow of the once blazing fire and stood there with Carolyn absorbing the radiant heat it still gave off. Staring into the red glow Stephen watched the festival of dancing heat whirling between the glowing vestiges of the yuletide log.

Turning around Stephen looked at the old couch next to the tree, which had faced the fireplace for over twenty years. It was an old couch they had purchased years ago from an estate sale of an older lady who had past away and whose children wanted the antique sofa to go to someone who would cherish it for the sentimental value it possessed versus the money it would fetch in an antique store.

It was a favorite spot for the young couple over the years as they laughed and cried on that couch. It was a resting spot where they laid the precious little bodies of their sleeping children during nap times and it was a place were they would lay when they were just tired and wanted to nap on a cool December night or on a hot July afternoon. It was more than a couch it was a friend, a comfortable, warm, enduring friend. Over the years it was given a new set of coverings to match changing times but the frame, its soul, never changed.

With Carolyn snuggled up in his arms Stephen lightly sat down on the antique sofa. He knew he could not take away her pain; all he wanted to do was to help her to forget about it, if only for a few moments. He picked up the remote on the end table and pointing it at the stereo system clicked the play button. Immediately the room was filled with the heavenly sound of Christmas music as if angels were literally pouring into their small living room singing the sacred hymns themselves.

Sitting on the couch with Carolyn curled up in her full length night gown, on his lap in an almost fetal position, Stephen stroked her hair with great gentleness, trying with each movement of his hand to ease the fear and suffering he knew she was enduring. Tenderly he pressed his lips on the top of her head and kissed her hair and forehead as she rested her tired head against his chest. With a gentle motion Stephen rocked ever so slightly side-to-side and softly hummed in accompaniment to the Christmas song that filled the room.

An hour or so had passed and sleep finally came to the eyes of Carolyn. Her mind had, for a short time, shut off the awareness of the ever-present pain and was allowing her to get some very needed sleep.

The sorrow Stephen felt at seeing the suffering his beloved wife was enduring was almost too much for his sensitive heart to handle. He wanted to cry out many nights in his prayers why God would allow his eternal companion to suffer so. He had made promises and bargains of things he would do if only she could be healed. He was good for his word. If he made a promise it was as good as done, so why wouldn't the Lord see fit to grant his petition?

He had sought special blessings of healing from the Lord's anointed over the years and was even willing to go as far as to the living prophet to plead his case for a blessing of healing for his wife, yet, it all seemed in vain. He had read the stories of scriptural miracles; the healing of the sick, Lazarus being raised from the dead, the blind given sight, the lame commanded to arise and walk, and the deaf made to hear!

Why did all the healings seem to happen two thousand years ago on a continent a thousand miles away and today, here and now, his Carolyn was fading away? Were miracles only reserved for a special few? Were they even granted to the common lot? Why did it seem as if these miracles only happened to the other guy?

Yet somewhere in the back of Stephens mind he knew all these feelings were part of an evolutionary process, maybe even a ride on an emotional roller coaster which took them from shock, to why me, to despair, to hope, to desperation, finally landing on unwelcome reality.

Stephen continued the slow rocking motion hoping the soft movement would continue to help Carolyn sleep. Beneath her chin was her tiny frail hand curled up in a tight fist. Stephen could feel with his hands the tightness of her grip. Gently stroking her hand she relaxed the tenseness and Stephen could feel that she had something buried within her fist. Feeling along the palm of her hand with his fingers he touched a hard circular object. Grasping it with his fingers he brought the object into the amber light of the fire and saw that it was a ring.

Tears welled up in Stephen's eyes as he stared at the simple old copper ring. A ring which to him had meant a great deal twenty-five years ago, but had increased in value a thousand times to Carolyn in the ensuing years. Holding the ring transported Stephen to a distant time when he was young, strong and full of dreams. A time when he was ready to grasp the

21

world by the reigns and ride it to riches and success. He chuckled slightly to himself as he remembered the frailty and the short sightedness of youth. Time had a way of teaching a man what it truly meant to be a man and it wasn't fame, fortune and free living.

It was on a cool summer night in a small northwestern town where he had first heard Carolyn's voice. He had never laid eyes on her but there was something magical in her voice as she spoke out of a second story window to a friend who had thrown pebbles at her window. Stephen had only been a passing actor on this late night stage; the real attraction was his friend, her boyfriend.

Several days later when they actually had the opportunity to meet, Stephen was even more enamored by Carolyn's charming personality and her wonderful beauty. Yet in her large dark eyes, which were the windows to her soul, was the real beauty.

After their brief encounter Stephen wasn't to see Carolyn for another five years. After a Romantic courtship and wonderful dates together Stephen felt he needed to propose the question of marriage. He knew he did not yet have the riches and wealth of his dreams; reality was that he had nothing and was only starting out on his journey of success.

He needed a ring in order to propose. After many disappointing trips to a plethora of jewelry stores and seeing the price tags Stephen knew he was not going to be purchasing one any time soon. In his desperation he fancied that this beautiful woman would treasure a homemade ring and would gladly accept of his proposal and would eternally cherish this ring. At least that is what his fanciful mind thought; deep in the recesses of reality he knew she would most likely laugh or be offended at his offer and that the ring would be a symbol of his failures past present and future.

Yet he had always been a risk taker and a dreamer so he decided to proceed with his design. Only recently had he decided to take a job as a plumber's apprentice. It sounded close enough to a magician's apprentice from King Arthur lore that he decided it would be a place to start. It didn't take long to realize that the imagined magic was just that, imaginary.

The Ring

Scouring through the copper bin in the shop where he worked was a collection of copper refuse from old job sites; he found a half inch piece of copper that looked shiny and new. He measured it out so it would be thin and dainty worthy of a beautiful hand. He cut the copper and over the next several days sanded and polished the copper ring until all the burrs and rough edges were gone and a smooth shiny finish emerged.

It wasn't an elaborate masterpiece quite the contrary it was extremely simple and very plain. Yet he felt that something within him was apart of this simple metal ring, his effort, his pure intent... his heart. After several visits to the jeweler's outside dumpster Stephen had found the perfect box, an elegant black velvet box with puffy white silk lining on the inside that a very well-to-do customer had thrown aside after removing her very ornate and expensive diamond ring.

Stephen placed the copper ring on top of the white silk and closed the black velvet lid and placed the homemade piece of jewelry in his pocket. Today was the day. He had it all planned out, a simple yet elegant dinner of sandwiches placed atop an elegant white paper plate, with a nice white tablecloth adorned with candles, napkins, and a silver butter dish into which he would place the ring. All of this would be held up by a beautiful borrowed folding card table in a mountain setting surrounded by pine trees, crisp air and puffs of snowdrifts.

When the moment was right he would put on a slow memorable song and then take her hand and ask her to dance on natures dance floor of pine needles and leaves. As they would sway to the magic of the music he would time it perfectly when he felt she was the most vulnerable; he would then make his way ever so casually to the silver butter dish on the dining table and with finesse and grace lift the lid and pop the question millions have asked throughout the ages with bated breath, "Will you marry me?"

Moments passed which seemed like a millennium to Stephen, "Yes," rang out the answer. It was that moment in time, which all the planets seem to halt in their revolution, and the sun stands still, and the moon falls from the sky. It is that miraculous moment when woman accepts man as her protectorate, her companion, her soul mate. Little did Stephen know at that instant what that simple copper ring would come to mean to Carolyn. She had worn the ring their entire marriage. Even though it made her finger green when the summer heat would cause her skin to sweat, even when Stephen had bought her a real wedding ring with a real diamond, she still wore the thin copper band alongside the gold band set with a diamond.

Here tonight at the end of life's journey Carolyn held the thin piece of copper in her tiny fist, while the gold band with the diamond, which was now too large to fit securely on her finger, sat on top of her night stand next to their wedding picture. Stephen placed the ring back in Carolyn's palm and delicately closed her fingers around the ring. Its value to her was now priceless.

The warmth of the fireplace, the hypnotizing effect of the lights, and the soft angelic melody of the Christmas music had caused sleep to once again come to Stephen's eyes. Carolyn, still curled up on his lap, was in a deep, almost anesthetic sleep, and did not move.

The cobble stone streets made it difficult to walk especially carrying a person. The sky was blue and the air hot and dry as Stephen walked down the steps of the narrow stone passageway toward an open area, which looked like some sort of a market place. He did not recall ever being in this place before yet it had a familiar feel to it almost as if he knew the place or had seen it some where or maybe even read about it.

Passing through the market place he was surprised at the number of people who were gathered there. It was as if some event or occasion or a celebration had taken place. Glancing around the plaza he heard people here and there talking about this man, who had the ability to command evil spirits to come out of people, and who it was rumored healed a blind man, and some even said raised a person who had been dead several days!

One woman, who was standing in front of Stephen, was even telling another how a woman she knew had been healed just by touching this mans garment. "No," came the exultant reply, as if to emphasis how amazing this was, and yet should be unbelievable.

The Ring

Almost as if in a stupor Stephen's head slowly turned as he looked around at his surroundings. The stone streets, the stone buildings, the high wall surrounding the city, a market place with figs and fish lying out on wooden tables, people in robes and sandals . . . where was he? He tried to clear his head by shaking it several times as well as to step on his toes with his other foot to see if this was real.

With aching toes he continued to shuffle through the crowd of people, Carolyn still in his arms. He paused at a merchants stand, and asked a person where they where and what had just happened here. The merchant looked at Stephen in an almost incredulous way and answered in a brusque manner, "Jerusalem!" Stephen stammered out the letters of the word trying to repeat what the man had just said, "J-e-r-u-s-a-l-e-m?" "Yes," came the response, "and the man from Galilee was just here preaching and healing some of the people. He does much good, but he also makes many enemies."

Stephen managed to ask if he was called Jesus? The man replied that he was and that he was glad that the heat had not caused permanent damage. Stephen asked where he might find this man? Pointing towards one of the gates of the city he let Stephen know he was most likely heading to one of the meadows near a hillside where he often taught the people.

Thanking him Stephen hurried as quickly as he could with his load down the dusty street towards the area the man had pointed to. After what seemed like a hundred miles in the heat and dust and carrying the extra weight, he found an area on a small hill where a crowd had gathered. His arms were burning, and his head ached from the physical strain, and his legs began to feel like jello left out on a hot sidewalk.

Approaching the group he could feel the sensation of peace and hope fill his heart. Standing on the outskirts of the crowd he could see a man speaking in the midst of the crowd, which was seated on the ground. The man's voice was not loud, he did not yell, it seemed that he was easily understood and his voice was powerful yet soft. Stephen realized this was indeed . . . Jesus, the very Christ, the Savior of the world.

Somehow, someway he had been transported through time and distance to the meridian of time and was now, here, on the outskirts of Jerusalem, listening to the Savior preach to the Jews. It couldn't be, yet here he was, and there was Carolyn lying in his arms, sick, frail, and dying.

Could miracles take on such miraculous condition? Was anything too hard for God? Was this the answer to his many desperate prayers pleading for the life of his wife? He didn't know, but what he did know was that at this moment in time he was here and Christ was there.

Where the time went he could not tell, but the sermon had ended and the crowd was beginning to disperse. The Savior with some of His disciples were also leaving. Stephen knew what he had to do; he had to make his way through the crowds of people to where Jesus going.

Desperately he hurried towards where he could see Jesus leaving through the throng of people. Pushing his way towards Him, stumbling on the uneven ground, weaving in-and-out of the masses, breathing in the dust made by a thousand feet, his arms so tired and the burning so intense that he was sure he could not keep going. With pain, weakness, and light-headedness, he continued to shuffle along with a determination to get to the King of Kings.

Losing his balance on a protruding root Stephen fell to one knee thrusting out one of his hands to the dirt of the earth to brace himself from a complete fall. He desperately held on to Carolyn so as not to make the fall jolt her excessively. He tried in desperation to get back up to pursue Jesus but his legs were so weak, his arms quivering, and his back aching with spasm, he knew he could not physically lift himself up, let a lone with Carolyn in his arms.

He watched the Savior and his disciples getting further away and in his extreme anxiety at loosing this precious opportunity he cried out, "Oh Jesus, please, please hear me, please, oh please help me, I need you, I need you …"

His voice trailed off as his head hung down on Carolyn's forehead.

All the months of feeling desperate, having to endure the feelings of loss and sorrow, and the heartache he felt at the illness of his companion, compounded by the feelings of abandonment by a loving God, and the overwhelming feeling of love for his wife, and his wish to spend many more years with her, all culminated in this moment and he lost all strength. Tears fell from his eyes to the dusty ground leaving minute indentions in the dirt. More than anything he had ever wanted, more than his own life, he wanted Carolyn to be healed. He could not live with out her! He knew he too would die, he knew he lacked the strength to live life alone.

Tears streaming from his eyes, shoulders trembling, arms burning, and legs weak he felt a hand rest upon his head. The touch of this hand filled his whole soul with warmth, almost as if light were penetrating into his muscles and soothing the ache and filling his whole body with this warmth of a touch. Another hand touched his chin and gently lifted up his head. Through the blur of tears he saw the kind and loving face of the Savior looking down at him. The love that penetrated from His eyes was astounding. His love was deep and considerate and of ancient date. Stephen could feel that Jesus knew him more thoroughly than he knew himself; he knew that the love he felt at that moment was genuine and real. It was so profound, so intense as to be overpowering.

"What wilt thou that I should do for thee?" came the voice of the Son of God, as he knelt down beside Stephen. The burning in his limbs, the weakness, the sorrow, the overpowering sorrow that he had felt . . .left, and with a voice trembling and choked with emotion he some how managed to let loose the words which were the deepest desire of his heart. "I want her," he replied, pointing with his eyes to the woman in his arms, "to be healed, she is sick, very very sick, and I . . . I do not want to loose her." The smile He gave Stephen was one of the most compassionate and empathetic gestures he had ever experienced. "My son, you will not loose her, she will be yours through out the eternities, the love you have for her will endure. You and her have been faithful."

He knelt down in front of Stephen and Carolyn and touched her head and in a quiet voice said be healed. Carolyn's body moved, her large dark brown eyes opened and brightness filled them like rays of light pouring into an opening through storm clouds. Stephen had never seen her eyes so bright before. She stood up from his lap alive filled with energy and vitality. Her skin and face were illuminated with a glow reminiscent of years past.

She looked at the Savior as He stood up and stepped toward her and embraced Carolyn within his loving arms. "Well done, Carolyn, thou hast been faithful." The experience was one that lacked the written word's ability to convey. Glancing up at them Stephen could not believe how well Carolyn looked. She had been healed; she was standing and smiling down at him.

Walking over to Stephen, Carolyn knelt down next to him and tenderly kissed him telling him how much she loved him and how grateful she was for his strength, his kindness, and patience during her illness. She told him how grateful she was to have spent her life with him and for all of the love, the laughter, and the fun times they had had. She expressed her undying love for their children and the wonderful life they had lived. He truly was her companion, her soul mate, her husband. She reached out and took his hand affectionately opening his fingers and placed a well-worn copper ring in the palm of his hand and then closed it, pressing his hand to her lips for a moment and then placed his strong hand lovingly back in his lap. She stood up and smiled at him once more and then bending over kissed him one more time on his forehead.

The warmth of the glowing coals, the lights from the tree and the subconscious awareness of the surrounding environment caused Stephen to wake up. There he sat on the antique couch, the lights from the Christmas tree casting a colorful hue around the small family room. Somewhat astonished he looked around the room as if trying to decide if this was really his home. But as it often does, reality came to him after a few dazed moments, and he realized he had been dreaming.

For a few moments he was amazed at how real the dream felt, the heat, the dust, the pain, the sorrow, the love, the Savior, the healing . . . He came to full awareness and felt Carolyn still curled up in his lap. Her frail body still felt light and cold, and she had not moved. Things seemed to be just as they were. She had not been healed, she was still sick. He bent forward and put his chin on her hair. He glanced down and saw that her hand had fallen, from where it had been curled tightly in a fist against his chest, to his lap, where it was open and lifeless. In her open palm was the simple copper ring he had made for her so many years ago with love.

Carolyn had passed quietly from mortality into the loving arms of her Savior while Stephen had gently rocked her on his lap dreaming of the reality of her return to her heavenly home. No, she had not been healed from her illness in this realm, she had finished her work, and a loving Father had given her and Stephen a few more months together and a few more special moments together to fill up the emptiness that would be in Stephen's heart. The Savior knew how much Stephen loved his wife and how badly he would miss her and felt enough compassion to allow her to linger a while longer.

Tears filled Stephens eyes as he realized his eternal mate had passed away in his arms on a Christmas Eve, the day before the celebration of the Savior who opened the door to eternal life for all those who would follow him. The Lord had given him the ability in a vision to see Carolyn released from her mortal tabernacle of pain and return into the loving arms of the Savior. He was allowed to see Carolyn one last time as a spirit before she left.

Today was Christmas; Stephen stood in front of their Christmas tree and looked at all the ornaments, which covered the branches that represented all the different places they had been together throughout their life. He savored the memories and offered a little pray of gratitude for having had the blessing of spending the last twenty-five years with the girl of his dreams.

He looked down at the palm of his hand to a little copper ring. Lifting it up to the light he twirled it around and around admiring, not the material it was made from, but what it signified. Tying a piece of thread through the ring he took one of the branches and placed the string from the little copper ring over one of the pine needles. Standing back a step or two he thought how beautiful it made the other ornaments on the evergreen tree look.

The Christmas Tradition

"Snow, why did it always snow on Christmas Eve," Jack thought? It was not that he did not like snow, exactly; it was, well, Christmas Eve. No one shoveled snow on Christmas Eve in all the storybooks he had read. But then, the world wasn't a storybook, at least not anymore.

Jack zipped up his heavy winter coat and pulled the knitted snowcap over his head as he grabbed the snow shovel adjusting the hat so it would cover his ears. He always hated how sensitive his ears were to the cold, especially when his neighborhood friend Del-Ray would flick his ears and then laugh as if his older brother were tickling his feet. Obviously, he did not realize how painful it was.

Bending over Jack pulled up the heavy wooden garage door exposing the white, wintery world the current storm was delivering. "Ominous" . . . he thought. The task ahead of him was "ominous". Not that Jack knew exactly what ominous meant, but he had heard his father use the word on several occasions when a task seemed larger and more difficult than what he had expected and tonight, it seemed that ominous best described his task perfectly. At least he liked the sound of it.

Digging the shovel deep into the snow, Jack began throwing the snow this way and that. "I wonder why there always seems to be snow drifts in the middle of the driveway," Jack thought, as he lifted another shovel full of snow onto the heap that was beginning to get high. He could feel the sweat begin to bead on his forehead. "It would seem to me," Jack muffled to himself, "that a snow drift would look much prettier if it were in the middle of the yard, where I wouldn't have to shovel it."

Resting on the handle of the shovel for a moment Jack noticed how large and bright the moon appeared. It seemed as if it had climbed down and sat on top of the majestic mountains that graced the view from their front yard. He had always seen pictures of the moon with a nightcap on and a smile gracing its face as if it were snuggled up in some warm flannel sheets having just been given a kiss goodnight by its mother. Somehow, it is what the image seemed to portray to his mind.

Jack noticed how gently the large snowflakes seemed to glide toward the earth. He raised his eyes toward the heavens and marveled at how many snowflakes there were, thousands, maybe millions of them journeying down to earth. "Angels," Jack thought, "I wonder how many angels it takes to cut out that many snowflakes." Each snowflake was a masterpiece of crystalline beauty, each unique, each carefully crafted to reflect the personality of the angel that had precisely cut out each one. He closed his eyes and felt each snowflake as it gently landed on his warm face, melting as quickly as the next one touched down.

The world seemed so peaceful and serene in winter. Especially in December as the sun set early to give way to the chill of the winter night. Yet to Jack it seemed a contradiction somehow.

Winter was the death of the year. It was the burial of spring and summer. And fall, fall was the last struggle before death silently covered its victim. Yet, tonight it seemed serene. "Yes," Jack thoughtfully pondered, "Serene."

A quick gust of wind blew across Jack's face stinging his nose and cheeks, leaving as quickly as it had come. "Hurry, yes I have to hurry and get the driveway done before father comes home," Jack mused to himself, as he snapped back to reality.

His dad had changed, a little more sad, but more than that, he seemed to be struggling against the weight of life's unforeseen trials. Grouchy, he was a little more grouchy, a little busier than he used to be, and expected a lot more from Jack than any other little nine-year-old boy. He demanded order and discipline. He expected that a chore be completed before he came home each evening. Nevertheless, little Jack did not dislike his father any less, as he understood the adjustment they both had to make to the new life they had been forced to live.

"Or Else," Jack pondered, " I wonder what "or else" was?" Jack considered thoughtfully, as he threw another heap of snow onto the pile that kept growing along the side of the driveway. Before his father left that morning he reminded Jack that he had better have the driveway done before he drove up that night, "or else!" "Or else," Jack thought again, and in a deep voice as if to mimic his father, "Or else we are going to have to make snow angels in the snow, or else we are going to have to have a snowball fight and conquer each other's snow castles!" Jack laughed, at the sight that thought conjured up in his mind.

"I wonder," Jack thought to himself again, "How is it that a snow flake can be so light and airy and float ever endlessly to the earth, and yet when millions of snow flakes congregate together on the ground they seemed to weigh a thousand pounds?" At least that is how heavy each shovel full of snow seemed to feel to Jack as he continued to work.

The driveway seemed to be longer than Jack remembered it. In summer, when he rode his stingray bike up into the garage to eat supper, it seemed so short. "Snow," Jack said, "snow always seems to make a thing look bigger." His little heart was beating hard in his chest and he could feel the muscles in his back burn as the task began to be arduous.

Thump, thump, thump, went the rhythm of his mother's heart as his little head lay on her chest. He could feel the rocking chair go forward and then back and forward again. It was their tradition. Every Christmas Eve his Mother would cradle him on her lap, rock him in the rocking chair, and gently stroke his hair with her warm, caressing fingers. The angelic sound of her voice sweetly singing his favorite Christmas song, which made him think the season would go on forever. The dancing of the lights on the walls as the fire flickered in the fireplace held Jack transfixed adding a warmth to the air that brought a cozy, surreal feel to the room.

"And in the days of Caesar Augustus . . . ," his dad would begin, as he read the Christmas story from St. Luke in the Bible. Each time his Father read the account of the Savior's birth, Jack thought of the little baby Jesus cuddled up in the arms of his sweet mother Mary and how warm and safe he must have felt. The thump, thump, thump, of Mary's heart must have been a lullaby, which put the infant child to sleep. "Life was wonderful, and always would be," he thought, as his father closed the Bible.

Crack, sounded the icicle as it fell from the roof and hit the driveway. "Almost done," thought Jack, grateful he did not have to do the sidewalks this time. As he shoveled the last bit of snow his breathing was heavy as if he had just beaten his best friend Jimmy in the one hundred-yard dash.

The heavy sound of his breathing carried Jack to a dark room filled with the sound of the strenuous effort to breathe. The air felt heavy as the nurse led Jack into the room with his father. "Do not ask her any questions that she will have to answer," the nurse had said, prior to going into the room, "only questions that she can nod her head yes, or no, to."

Jack knew that his mother was sick and even accompanied her on several occasions to the big hospital as she underwent treatments. Nevertheless, he always knew she would get better in a few days just as Jack did when she lovingly cared for him when he had come down with the chicken pox.

Somehow, as he walked hesitantly to the bed where she lay, Jack could feel the tears roll down his little cheeks and into the corners of his mouth, "why was I crying?" he thought, afraid he would have to answer his own question. He could sense it was not going to be all right. "Hello Pumpkin," she whispered gently, yet with the greatest of effort.

Jack always felt embarrassed when she called him pumpkin, a nickname given to him when he was a baby that somehow stuck. However, tonight it landed on Jack's ears as manna on the dewy ground in the morning. Her hand reached up and took his little hand in hers and gently she soothed his fears. Those hands, how fragile, how frail they looked. The needles and tubes running from those delicate hands to those big machines. Those hands, that were always so gentle yet strong. Those hands that bandaged up his scraped knees, those hands that wrapped so firmly around him after he had been lost in the department store. Those hands that ever so gently wiped away the tears from his eyes after Skip the neighborhood bully told him he was a sissy, those hands that caressed his hair each Christmas eve in the rocking chair. How thin, how frail they looked.

Jack could hardly breathe, his fears were running away with him, how he wanted to jump on the bed and hold her tight, so tight that no one could take her. However, he knew, he could not. The tubes that ran down her nose, the monitors that crowded her bed were as barriers to Jack, barring the way. Yet, her eyes seemed to speak to his the soft, sweet message of "I love you."

The gentle wind froze the tears to his cheeks as he realized he had finished the job. He turned to see the lights of the Christmas trees that adorned the windows of the houses in his neighborhood. As he walked toward the garage, he could see the multi colored prisms that reflected in the snow from a thousand different Christmas lights. As Jack hung up the snow shovel he realized, it had been over a year since his mother had passed away. It had forced him to grow up. It was time to put away little boy things and be a man.

He hung his wet coat on the nail in the garage and pulled off his wet gloves. He examined his fingers trying to warm them up and alleviate the stinging. "That's another thing," Jack mumbled to himself, "why do finger's wrinkle up when they are wet?" Neatly he set his snow boots in the corner next to the kitchen door. Father will be home any minute and he knew he had to get the soup ready so they could enjoy the holidays.

"What would you like for Christmas?" the department store Santa Clause had asked him, as Jack reflected back on their recent visit. Jack looked around the big store and realizing he could not give him, what he really wanted. "A slinky," he said quietly, as he quickly crawled off Santa's knee.

Jack set the table neatly putting each spoon in its place, and filling up the glasses with water. Jack was done, now he just had to wait for his father's arrival.

Jack went to his room. He knew what he wanted for Christmas. He knelt quietly down on his bony little knees, burying his head deep into his pillow. Jack began to sob. "Dear Heavenly Father, please let my mother know that I miss her. And please, wish her a Merry Christmas." He hesitated for what seemed like an eternity, knowing what he wanted more than anything else, he knew what his Christmas wish was. However, he was afraid to ask, feeling as if asking would negate the wish all together. Yet he knew it was his wish. "Please, dear Father," Jack's voice began again, trembling, "let our tradition happen just once more. Let me hear the sound of my mother's heart once more, please, let me feel her gentle hands run through my hair and her sweet voice whisper in my ears, just once more."

"Son, you've done a great job with the meal, and thank you for doing your chores today," his father said. "I'm proud of you. And I know your mother is too." As Little Jack leaned into his father's chest, he knew his father loved him, and he knew he loved his mother. Jack knew all would be well.

Jack could hear his father's door shut as he went to bed. He was tired, not just tired because he worked hard, but tired deep down in his soul. Jack pushed the covers off him and quietly crept over the floor and down the stairs. He stood for a moment amazed at the lights of the Christmas tree. The quiet aura of the season filled the room. Slowly he sat down in the old rocking chair, bringing his knees up to his chest, forward, and back, forward, and back he rocked. The dancing lights of the fire hypnotizing his thoughts. Reverently he leaned his head back onto the chair. Closing his eyes, and feeling the sensation of the rocking chair gently moving, backward and forward.

Thump, thump, thump, echoed the sound of the beating heart in his mother's chest. He felt her warm hand touch his head, her caressing fingers running through his light brown hair, combing them ever so softly. Her angelic voice singing the sweet Christmas hymn he had loved so much. He felt her tender lips touch his closed eyes as she gave him sugar kisses. "I have missed you my little pumpkin," she whispered, in his small ear. "I love you, and Merry Christmas. I will always be watching you." Jack had never been so warm, and peaceful in his entire life, her being radiated her love through every part of his being like sunshine in the morning. How Jack wished she could stay, How he missed her, oh how he missed her so very much.

Jack felt a prickly kiss on his cheek and big arms scoop him up. "Let's get you to bed pumpkin," he heard the voice of his father, whisper in his ear.

Jack had been given his Christmas wish. A little boy, who maybe wanted something so much, and had faith enough, that he could not be kept from within the Veil?

The strong hands reverently closed the storybook, his fingers rubbing gently the raised letters bearing the words, Journal- Volume I. Jack looked up from the sofa where he was seated; a peaceful hush filled the air. The flickering lights of the fire created dancing shadows on the walls, and the Christmas tree all lit up with multi-colored lights, snow flakes hanging from the branches of the tree, graced by the angel overlooking the entire room from her perch atop the decorated tree.

The golden hues on little James' face gave him a warm, protected appearance. His head bent over Jack's elbow, eyes closed tightly, and mouth open with a purring little sound. Jack leaned over, kissed his little cherubim cheeks, and glanced over at the cuddled up bundle on the end of the sofa.

Mächen, his sweet little Mächen, her bunny slippers curled up tightly together looking as peaceful as did she. "Snow flakes, her face was as angelic as snow flakes," Jack thought, with a smile.

And Michael, my little, big Michael, curled up in the rocking chair, his mother gently running her fingers through his hair, softly kissing his closed eyes. "In a couple more years he will be more independent," he thought, "but tonight, tonight he would be his mother's little pumpkin."

"Oh," said Jack, quietly to his wife Carolyn, "how grandmother would have loved to cuddle, and rock these little ones." The tender smile radiating from Carolyn's face let Jack know she understood.

As Jack tucked the last precious bundle in bed, kissing his lovely wife goodnight, he went downstairs and slipped into the rocking chair. The shadows of the fireplace still danced around, and the lights of Christmas filled the silent room. "Time," Jack thought, "does it ever take a vacation or go on a break, or get tired and slow down?" "Probably not," he said, answering his own question, "but it does heal all wounds."

How the years had passed. How the hurt had turned to joy. He reverently laid his head back against the rocking chair, and rocked back, and forth, back, and forth, wishing again, just one more time, for that special Christmas tradition.

Thump, thump, thump, went the beating of her heart . . .

The Christmas That Never Was

As I sit by the warmth of the crackling fire, the shadows of the Christmas tree lights blinking on the white walls of the family room, I find my mind wandering back to a time when I was a boy. The soft sound of soothing Christmas music fills the air and the sound of the crackling fire fills in the spaces between the notes of the melodic sound.

Someone once said that lucky is the person who has many friends, but truly blessed is the person who has one true friend. So I would count myself blessed. It was thirty-eight years ago that this unique friendship was born. It passed through childhood fun, teenage mischief, young adult adventure, adult responsibility, and many many memories. To chronicle the friendship would take volumes and would probably not be able to capture the essence of what this friendship truly was.

I find myself this Christmas season sitting in a surreal state as memories flood into my mind from Christmases long past. The excitement of sharing, with a good friend, what jolly ole Saint Nick had delivered to each of our homes, and then playing with each other's toys while exchanging Christmas wishes.

Odd enough is the memory of the Christmas that never was. Sitting with my head laid back on the leather headrest of my sofa I sip on a cup of hot chocolate in between the memories that flood into my mind. The events of that Christmas that never was pour onto the stage of my mind as vivid as it did then. It mixes reality with dreams, verity with visions, and fact with fiction.

It was a Christmas that I know I never physically experienced, but the events were so real I struggle at times to believe it was only a dream. It must have existed somewhere between the moonlight of night and the rising of the golden sun of day, or between the world of sleep and the world of the awake. I could touch and smell that world around me. Maybe it was the land where Peter Pan lived?

It happened several years ago as life ebbed slowly away and two souls were on the edge of change. It was a final adventure that had a profound effect on two people whose paths were at the crossroads of separation. To you the reader, I will try and illuminate it in such a way as to help you find joy in the meaning of Christmas this season and in all your Christmas seasons to follow. For that is what happened to me.

Life is a paradox of opposites. A place where love and hate coexist, where light and dark chase each other, where happiness and sorrow intertwine, where truth and lies compete, and where health and sickness exchange places. So it was with our lives. The path of my life followed a set of trials and experiences, and my friends followed a different path of trials and experiences. His path was strewn with illness.

If you had seen him as a teenager your opinions would have not come to the conclusion what life ended up choosing for him. You would have thought him athletic, full of ability and vigor, and a love for life and adventure. He laughed, loved, and lived. But the wheel of time turned and a different set of cards were dealt. His was a life of illness with three phases of struggles, two of which he battled valiantly for many seasons and became the victor, and the third he battled for a short season and was vanquished.

The unwelcome news came as he approached his quinquagenarian time of life, which is to say his fiftieth year. He had battled colitis which ended up with his colon being removed and a new one created via a new procedure. Then the wheel of time turned and now he battled liver failure due to bile ducts becoming plugged. He ended up undergoing a liver transplant. In each case the wheel of time turned and cancer was detected. In each case he fought the fight and conquered. The final turning of the wheel brought with it cancer this time in his kidneys. Hector, the hero of the Trojan War, who fought valiantly, finally became weary of the endless battle with Achilles of Mycenae, and was slain. Rome, the great nation that ruled the world for a thousand years was finally weakened by internal and external strife. Finally she fell to the Goths never to rise from the dust again. So it was with my dear friend, weary of too many years of suiting up for battle and wielding the metaphoric sword in his defense, he became weary of the battle, the internal strife of his health, and was finally vanquished.

The Christmas That Never Was

It was the Christmas of his fiftieth year. He lay in a hospital bed withering away from the cancer waiting for the emissaries of the next life to call his name and welcome him back home. I sat at his bedside in an embrace that confirmed a lifetime of friendship. Through the strength of my embrace I wanted to convey love and comfort to a soul brought down with sorrow. I could almost wrap my arms twice around his now boney frame. Tears filled our eyes as we communicated without words. Feelings, memories, and experiences now were the unspoken words.

Rest had finally overtaken James, my lifetime friend, and his body relaxed. It was while I sat next to his bed during this time that the most amazing Christmas experience we had ever known happened.

The sun set early on that short December day. The crispness of the cold could be seen on the hospital window. It was almost as if the biting cold of winter wanted to break through the glass and fill the room with its icy cold tentacles. The night light above the bed gave off a dim illumination that filled my friends face with just enough light to see the visible pain still etched on his sleeping face. The inability of the tiny light to travel the distance of the room left the remainder of the room in a dark shade of gray. The blinking L.E.D. lights of the monitors and life sustaining equipment flashed on the walls much like the lights of my Christmas tree do now as I rest my head against the back of my sofa next to the warmth of the fire.

As I watched the almost unknown face of my friend, my eyes became heavy with sleep. I had been awake for many hours and could feel the arms of sleep wrapping themselves around me. The inevitable struggle against sleep finally came and I succumbed. If I were awake, I would have found myself asleep with my head on his bed and my body precariously relaxed half in the chair and half out of the chair.

It was while I was in this balanced state that the room began to fill with an exceedingly bright light. Through my closed eyelids I could see the brightness increase until I finally felt obliged to open my eyes. The brightness was blinding and I found that my arm was shielding my face from its intensity. I leaned back in the chair still unsure of exactly what was happening. I looked up at the ceiling where the florescent light was but it was not on. Perplexed I looked around for the source of the intense light and could not find it.

I slowly stood, my hand still trying to shield my eyes, and moved to the foot of the bed. Standing there for a second I felt the presence of a person and spun around partially startled, to find my friend, James, standing there with a smile on his face. I stared at him wondering what he was doing out of bed. I was about to rush over to him and insist he climb back in bed as he was in no condition to be standing when I noticed that he looked radiant, full, and healthy. I stuttered some incoherent tones as my mind was trying to form a sentence with a question mark at the end of it.

He moved closer and then touched my arm and said that it was time to go and have our Christmas adventure. I sputtered a response querying what he was talking about when he pointed to another person who had entered the room. The visitor was dressed all in white and shone with the same intensity as the light around us. James led me over to the visitor in white. Standing in front of him, my mind whirling with questions, he held out both of his hands conveying to us to take his hand.

Without a questioning thought I reached out and held his hand at the same time my friend did. Within a flash we were whisked from the brightness of the hospital room and traveled upwards toward a bright moon and a starry sky that dotted the darkness of the night. I looked downwards and saw the lights of the city getting smaller and smaller as the brisk breeze of the night air fluttered through my hair and past my face.

I looked back up at the visitor in white and saw that he was silent and intent on guiding us on this midnight sail among the stars. My mind was not grasping any of this. I could feel his hand still holding mine and saw his other still holding that of my friend. Looking over at James I saw the breeze brushing past him as well, his face lit up with a bright smile of hope and freedom. He was flying and looked as if he felt right at home up here in the starry night sky.

Just about the time I started to fully realize what was happening and to feel fright at flying high in the night sky with a man illuminated in white

I found myself standing in a field. The air was not cold, neither was it hot, but was warm and dry. I looked around the field, which was situated on a slight hill, and saw a bunch of sheep scattered around grazing. It was still night, but the heavens seemed brighter than I would have thought for this time of night. Still scanning the hillside meadow I saw scrubby trees sparsely dotting the landscape along with rocks and boulders scattered here and there.

My eyes continued to peruse the landscape when I saw half a dozen men a hundred yards or so ahead of me gazing up at the sky. I was taken back by what they were wearing. It appeared as if they were still in their bathrobes standing in the middle of a field. I followed their upturned heads into the sky and saw the most magnificent star whose brightness was beyond any other star I have ever beheld. It was many times larger than any other star in the sky. The aureola of light that surrounded the star illuminated outwards from its center and extended through its four apparent points shooting out into the night.

Standing there looking at this illuminated phenomenon I glanced over to my friend and saw that he too was amazed at the sight of this star. I'm not sure how long we stood there gazing heavenwards but the feeling that permeated our soul was indescribable. We knew that this star had a special meaning.

"Where are we," I asked James, as I looked around trying to put some sense to the unfamiliar landscape. "I'm not sure," he answered, "but lets see if we can find out." "Lets talk with those men over there," he said, pointing to the men in bathrobes. I acknowledged my agreement with a nod of my head and began walking towards them.

Walking over the rocks and through the golden grass the place seemed strangely familiar, as if I had seen this place before. As we got closer to the men James looked at me and with a curious look on his face said, "Do you recognize who these men are?" We both stopped and staring at them I answered with a tone of disbelief, "They, they look like shepherds?" "Yes," he replied, "but look close, they are shepherds that we've seen in pictures from a long time ago."

Indeed, they wore cotton robes with cloth headpieces and simple leather sandals. They had a shepherds crook in their hands and they were standing gazing upwards surrounded by sheep unaware that we were less than ten yards away. I was about to call out to them when all of a sudden a bright light, independent of the incredibly bright star, descended from the skies and shone on the ground. The light enveloped the shepherds and within that light we saw a man standing who was also illumined wearing a white robe his arms, feet, and upper chest bare.

We fell to our knees unsure of where we were or what was happening. I suppose we didn't want to be spotted by anyone, as if we were not really suppose to be here. At the appearance of the visitor the shepherds stepped back holding up their hands as if to cover their eyes and as if attempting to protect themselves from the unknown. They seemed as if they were afraid of the personage. In a voice, like the rushing of water, the heavenly visitor spoke to the gathered shepherds. "Fear not: for, behold, I bring you good tidings of great joy, which shall be to all people. For unto you is born this day in the city of David a Saviour, which is Christ the Lord. And this shall be a sign unto you; Ye shall find the babe wrapped in swaddling clothes, lying in a manger."

To say we were dumbfounded would be an understatement. Like a lightening bolt striking hard in a storm filled night, the realization of what was happening flooded into our minds. It was unfathomable! Now, lying on our backs on the ground I looked over at James and started to speak when he said, "We are in Bethlehem at the time of Jesus' birth!" His voice sounded like I felt, completely bewildered. "How on earth did we…" my voice trailed off, as all of a sudden there was a multitude of heavenly angels surrounding the angel who had delivered the message of the birth of the King of the world.

The entire host of angels began to praise God, raising their voices in reverential tones and in unison cried out, "Glory to God in the highest, and on earth peace, good will toward men." The feelings that permeated to the very center of our beings were indescribable. A feeling of warmth and light filled our hearts and our minds as we listened to angels from the presence of God praise Him and His newborn son. We laid there in stunned silence.

Moments passed and the angels ascended upwards into the heavens and the funnel of light withdrew following the angelic host upwards until all had vanished and the sky again was dark except for the brightness of the new star. James' face was aglow with the after affect of the intensity of light, and with conviction said, "It is all true! I mean the Christmas story in Luke, the shepherds, the visit of the angel, the heavenly host singing and praising God, it is all true! I always knew it was! I knew this all really happened!" Looking at me he said, "and we are here, here in a field with shepherds near Bethlehem witnessing the announcement that the baby Jesus has been born."

I was about to declare the same emotions of amazement when we heard the shepherds say to each other, "Let us now go even unto Bethlehem, and see this thing which is come to pass, which the Lord hath made known unto us." They communicated amongst themselves choosing a couple of the shepherds to stay with the flocks while the others would follow the star to the manger promising to report back with every detail of what they had found.

Looking at each other with wordless communication James and I rose to our feet and scrambled closer to the shepherds so we could follow them to the manger. The sound of the rustling of grass startled them again and they turned and saw the two of us coming near. We called out that we meant no harm and had also heard the voice of the angel and likewise wanted to follow the star to Bethlehem. With out stretched arms they embraced James and I and welcomed us to join them in their short pilgrimage to the place below the star. "Come," said the eldest of the shepherds, "we must hurry."

My heart pounded so heavily within my chest that I felt anyone looking at my shirt would be able to see it pulsating. I was here in the old world at the end of an era, and at the beginning of a new era. I was here at the transition from B.C. to A.D. I was following the holy star to the babe in Bethlehem. Chills ran up and down my spine pronouncing themselves all over my arms. I looked at James, with a shepherds arm around his

45

neck, a smile gracing his face, and knew he was feeling the same chills I was. Together we were seeking out the babe in the manager.

My mind filled with memories spanning decades of us seeking to find and follow that same little babe. But, more than that, we had sought to follow that babe who had grown up and became a man, a divine man who had been lifted up on a cross for all men to see, so all could come unto Him and be healed from sin and sorrow, like the brazen serpent raised high in the air by Moses so that the people of Israel good look and live. And now, this Christmas season, here we were, two friends, fellow followers of the Christ, in a field with shepherds, once again seeking out the Christ.

After walking with haste through the grassy fields of the hillside and a long a dusty, rocky road we came upon a small village dotted with little houses made from sticks and stones. The light of the star shone bright over the tiny village and soon we where in the center of Bethlehem. People were still milling about and the town seemed packed with people and animals. Sounds of revelry and animals could be heard coming from some of the inns.

The shepherds had stopped to ask a few people in the street what direction the light was shining from. They pointed towards the hillside and said there were some stables up there, and in one of them, lying in a manger, was a baby. Thanking them the group of shepherds made their way through the narrow dusty streets keeping their eye upon the beams of light the star emanated until we came upon an opening and could see a short way off a cave of sorts cut into the hillside. The intense light seemed to be signaling that this was the spot where the babe could be found.

The pace of the shepherds slowed as they neared the location of the light from the star. Instead of slowing down my heart seemed to escalate throbbing so hard as to be almost unbearable. One hand on my chest the other instinctively reached out and grabbed James by the arm. I squeezed it as we drew near to the manger. Both of us looked at each other as if to say, "Can this really be happening?" Reaching a wooden gate one of the shepherds lifted up the latch and swung open the gate which led into the manger. The night was calm, quietness pervaded the air, and the lifting of the latch and the creaking of the gate invaded the quiet and to the stillness of the night sounded like an army of men rushing into battle.

We all reverently entered through the gate and there, engulfed in a beam of warm light, seated on the hay, surrounded by cattle, sheep, donkeys, and chickens were a dark haired man with a full beard clothed in a robe and headdress, and a serene, lovely young woman holding a new born baby. It was Joseph and Mary and cradled in Mary's arms was the King. I could hardly breath. I felt as if I wanted to melt. The shepherd's knelt down in front of the young couple and bowed their heads and paid their respect to this King of kings. As if to communicate to us to come forward, the shepherds had all knelt to one side or the other of the make-shift wooden crib.

With humility and awe, James and I walked slowly forward to the edge of the crib and knelt down in front of it. Our eyes made contact with those of Mary and Joseph and an intense feeling of faith filled our hearts. Mary looked down and with one hand unwrapped the swaddling clothes that enveloped the tiny baby Jesus and revealed His face and His tiny body to us. He was curled up asleep in the protective arms of His mother. Her face shone with love and kindness for her newborn son. We gazed upon the child with the utmost reverence, admiration and veneration.

There we were, kneeling in front of the Savior of the world. A child that would grow in the grace of God, His Father. A child that would increase in wisdom and stature and in favor with God. A child that would grow to be the Christ. A Savior who would save us all from sin and death. A Savior who would invite all of us to come unto Him so He could take upon Him our yoke and lighten our burdens. There we were, and we had no gift to give the King. A feeling of shame began to pervade our emotions. Before the negative thought could take root a tidal wave of understanding flooded into our minds and said, "All that the Son of Man requires is a broken heart and contrite spirit. He wants your faith and your heart."

The words were warm inside our minds and warmed our hearts as we knew we were all to willing to give to our King our faith, our hearts, and our love. We had already committed long ago to be followers of the word and to keep His commandments and to serve Him. Both of us had the burning testimony that He was the way, the truth, and the life.

The experience was so overwhelming that tears filled my eyes as I beheld my King. I knew what he would do for me and for all mankind. I knew the suffering He was to endure, the pain, the agony, the betrayals. And yet, I knew He would do it out of love for me, for me and for all my fellow man. I glanced over at my good friend and saw the tears that rolled down his cheeks splashing onto the ground moistening the dirt surrounding the mother and child. We looked up into the eyes of Mary and saw compassion and light. She knew who her son was. She knew who His Father was. She knew He was divine. Her eyes communicated understanding of what we were experiencing and felt joy that some of mankind would indeed know that Jesus is the very Christ.

I put my arm around James' shoulder as we knelt there and quietly said, "Merry Christmas Jim." He patted my knee and with emotions that welled up inside of him managed to whisper, "Merry Christmas to you too my old friend. I will miss you. Thank you for sharing this wonderful Christmas experience with me." As I was about to respond I lifted my head and looked about a dark room slightly aglow with a tiny LED light pulsating from a monitor. Startled I looked about the room I was in and saw that my good friend was asleep in the hospital bed with a myriad of tubes and hoses still connected to him.

"It was a dream?" I incredulously whispered out into the silent room. "I fell asleep at the side of the bed and I dreamed all of this?" My mind whirled about with the incredible realism of the dream. How was it possible? Sadness filled my heart as I realized it was just a dream, one that I alone was able to enjoy. I stood up by the bedside of my friend and with a tear of sadness rolling down my cheek place my hand on my friend's chest and felt the slight beating of his heart. I knew that in a very short time that beating heart would be stilled and he would be gone. He would leave this world and would open the door into the next. I knew it would be many years before we would be able to embrace one another in friendship again.

The Christmas That Never Was

The quiet, dry, crackling voice of my friend filled the air of the silent room. I looked at his face and saw that his eyes were filled with moisture, almost to the point of overflowing, he was trying to speak. Moistening his dry throat he reached out grabbing my hand that was on his chest and said in a very weak voice, "We saw Him, we saw the babe. We always knew He was real. It was the best Christmas ever." He squeezed my hand with what little strength he had and then closed his eyes and drifted of into sleep again. Gazing at his face I did not see the pain etched in it as I had done earlier that evening, but I saw peace. His face had a glow about it and almost looked as if it were full of color and life. I sat back down in the chair and reflected on the Christmas that never was.

I opened my eyes again to see the once raging fire gone and the embers glowing red in the fireplace of my family room. The melodic Christmas music that filled the air had stopped and the lights of the tree were still blinking on the white walls. The collar of my shirt was moist and my mind was filled with the joys of Christmas. Of all the Christmases that I had spent with my once and good friend, the surreal experience of a manger in Bethlehem still stands out as the preeminent experience of what Christmas is truly about.

I stood up from my comfortable chair, and walked over to the blinds of my family room window and parting them looked out onto a field of freshly fallen snow. It was all incandescently lit up from a full moon that hung in a cloud filled sky and shone brightly, almost like a star two thousand years ago. I bowed my head and offered a silent prayer of gratitude for friendship, for memories, for wonderful experiences, and for the Christ child who grew up to be the Christ, and for all He had done for me so I could one day open that door and return with my family and once again see a good ole friend.

The Book

The screech of the plane's tires hitting the runway brought Jason back to reality. He had been staring out the tiny oval window of the plane not really seeing the scenery thirty-two thousand feet below, nor the clouds that surrounded the plane. The world around him seemed surreal and distant knowing his father had passed away.

He had received a text message from his sister, who lived an hour away from his father, in a small town just north of where he grew up. She lived there with her husband and three small children. She had called him several times with the sad news but receiving no answer she decided to send him a text. It had come as a surprise to him. He was sitting in a meeting surrounded by corporate managers and subcontractors and was unable to answer his sister's call. However, reading the text message his sister had sent, he sat there stupefied for several moments. Everyone around the conference table stared at him waiting for an answer to a question that had been asked. He was oblivious that a question had even been asked.

"Jason, is everything all right?" Came the response. "Uh, no, not really," was the ambiguous reply. "I need to go," he said, as he stood stuffing papers into the pockets of his leather shoulder bag. Everyone just stared as he turned and left the room.

As Jason grabbed his bag from the overhead compartment his thoughts once again turned to the surprising news. He wondered how it could be that somehow we think everyone will live forever. We just go about our days involved in our lives not giving a second thought to anyone else around us and what might be happening in their life. It seemed especially so for parents who had raised their children and who now had children of their own. We just assume our parents are there and are doing what ever it is that they do, and that they will just keep on doing that indefinitely.

Then, once the unexpected news comes, we are surprised. Only then do we begin to think about that person and what must have been happening in their lives. So it was with Jason. He had realized that somehow time had just elapsed at a much faster rate than what he had realized. "Where had the years gone," he thought, as he stepped onto the shuttle bus that would take him to the car rental facility.

The flakes of snow that were small and almost unnoticeable earlier were now falling in large flakes and we're sticking to the windshield of the car as he sped towards his father's home. Night had fallen quickly on this twenty-second day of December. In three days it would be Christmas. "Some Christmas," he thought. The funeral would be held in two days and most likely his two sister and two brothers were already at his father's house.

Most of his brothers and sisters lived within and hour or so from his fathers home. He was the only one who had moved half way across the country. He really wasn't sure if it was because he had gotten a good job offer with a construction company as a project manager or if it was because he had simply grown apart from his father, and from his other siblings for that matter.

For some reason he had thought of himself as different somehow from the rest of the brood. He didn't really follow their religious beliefs, political views, or values, per se. He just felt differently then they did. Now, he had been gone almost twenty years. In all that time he had returned home to visit maybe twice. His father had faithfully sent him birthday and Christmas cards each year. He even called him several times throughout the year, but always had to leave a message.

Jason turned on his blinker and watched as the light from the orange bulb illuminated the snow that was now sticking more heavily on the ground. This was the street that he had grown up on. His father and mother had moved into this house when he was eight years old and his father never left. He wondered why life had turned out as it did? That thought was followed up by the thought "Did it have to turn out that way?"

Well, whichever way it was, it was at this point, what it was, and there was no going back in time to change things. It would be awkward, he was sure, seeing his siblings and their families, some of whom he had never seen in person before.

The Book

He pulled the keys out of the ignition and just sat in the driveway resting his head on the headrest staring up at the blinking icicle Christmas lights that dangled from the overhang of the porch. Sitting there contemplating he remembered the many Christmases he had experienced as a child in that house. One by one his mind remembered them all. The songs they had sung, the ornaments on the tree, the chocolate advent calendar they fought each other over to open, the gifts that were ripped open with enthusiasm, and the food that made the day special.

These memories were sweet to his soul. He loved how it had felt when they were all together at Christmastime. Somehow the differences that he felt now seemed so far away back then. As he opened the door to the car he felt a rush of cold air bite against his face. What would it be like now that the season of sweet memories was upon him, only this time, death was the reason he would be walking through the front door.

His oldest sister Jessica answered the door. "Jason," she cried, with warm enthusiasm and genuineness. She hugged him as he stepped back into his childhood home. As she hugged him his eyes took in the old home that was filled with memories. The warm glow of the lights from the family room just around the corner sent residual light into the entryway lighting up the room in a pale yellow.

The old piano still graced the center of the front room, the painting of George Washington praying at Valley Forge still hung above the piano, and the antique golf balls in the glass case still hung above the old hickory set of clubs leaning in the corner. The visual experience brought a hollow pang in his stomach.

"Is everyone here," he asked Jessica somewhat hesitantly; as she released him from her hug and placing the palm of her hand on his cheek. She had always been the caring, concerned, loving older sister. His mother had died when he was thirteen and his sister had naturally assumed the role and had loved him just like a mother. It had been hard for him. Somehow it had changed him, changed his heart and his thoughts.

Maybe he felt God had no right to take her, or maybe God didn't care about the life of some thirteen year old kid, or maybe, there just wasn't a

53

God. Whatever it was, it had altered the course of his life. Yet throughout his personal struggles Jessica had always been there for him. Many times acting as a buffer between him and his father who struggled to understand why he acted as he did and became the man he did when he was taught so differently.

"Yes, they are all in the family room. The children are all in bed. Actually, everybody is except Janet, Jake, and Jer." For some reason his parents had decided that a family of alliteration was the thing to do. So the siblings in order were, Jessica, Jake, Jason, Janet, and Jeremiah, but everyone called him Jer for short. His mother's name was Jenny and his father's name was James. And, of course, their last name had to be Johnson. So there it was, the seven J's of the Johnson's.

Jason felt anticipation, probably with a mixture of anxiety thrown in as he walked around the corner and down the two steps into the family room where all of his siblings sat. The scene seemed like one out of a Norman Rockwell painting. There was the evergreen Christmas tree all bedecked with garland, lights, tinsel, varied ornaments, and a white angel on top to oversee the festivities of the season. Below the branches of pine needles raced a replica of the Polar Express clicking on the tracks as it circled the tree. A warm crackling fire blazed in the fireplace and seven red stockings with white cuffs hung on the mantle awaiting the jolly man in red to come down the chimney.

There sat Janet curled up in the lazy boy in her red Rudolf pajamas, with white furry slippers. Jake was sitting on the floor leaning against the couch decked from head to toe in flannels, and Jeremiah was stretched out on the couch with moms old Christmas quilt covering his medium sized frame.

When he entered they all stood and welcomed him home to the place where all the memories began. If there was any awkwardness it was on the part of Jason as his heart had forgotten how good and kind his brothers and sisters were and how they had all grown and bonded together after the passing of their mother. Jason alone had chosen a different road to let his emotions travel down.

It had been a long time, a really long time. He was taken back in time in his memories of what their old home used to be like. No one had really changed, maybe they all simply grew up. He was the one who had changed, not only physically, but in another way as well, he couldn't put his finger on it exactly, or how to describe it. For those who understand the spirit of Christmas they would describe it as a spiritual change, or a spiritual maturity. They had all grown in their spiritual beliefs and understanding of what Christmas was really about.

It wasn't the eight reindeer pulling a sleigh with a plump old man in a red suit. It wasn't presents or gingerbread houses or elves at the North Pole, or wreaths on the door. It was about a baby born in Bethlehem who grew up and healed the sick, made the blind to see, the deaf to hear, and raised the dead. It was about that man without sin who bled in a garden, died on a cross, and rose again from a tomb.

Jason had missed all of this. He had lived his life as if this babe had never been born. He wasn't even aware anymore that he bled for him, hung on that cross for him, and left the tomb empty for him. His spiritual life had stalled out. By choice he had put his spirituality on a shelf neatly tucked into a box all taped up and secure.

Being in that room he felt the stark difference without anyone saying a word or pointing out the obvious to him. The feeling that permeated the room was a resplendent warm sensation that made his emotions tingle. "Why did I leave? What was my young mind thinking? Why was I filled with such frustration, anger, bitterness, and resentment?"

This feeling he was now feeling, as he stood there in the old family room, filled with family, is what he had felt on all of the Christmases past. It was the feeling his mother created, the feeling his father had perpetuated, and four siblings had passed on to the next generation.

Jason sat in the old wooden rocker that was between the Christmas tree and the fireplace. His brothers and sisters and himself talked about their father and about his life and memories they all shared in common with him and memories they individually had. They spoke about what memories they could remember about their mother. It had been so long ago that those memories took a little more effort to pull out. The older siblings had more memories and were able to share lost memories with the younger siblings who were comparably younger when their mother had passed away. They talked about memories they shared between them as siblings and memories they had shared one on one with each other.

Sitting in the family room, which was all decorated for the season, much of their memories turned to memories of Christmas time. In the Johnson household the holidays were a big deal. Jenny had tried to make the holidays a special time and focused it on families. Each month of the year had a holiday or special day of some sort and they made it a day of decorations, activities, and family together time. For the one month of the year where there was no holiday, August, they made up a holiday, Jintabuline Day. It celebrated the letter J and all things that were named or called with a J such as juniper trees, Joshua crossing into Canaan, Jack and Jill going up the hill, Jesters and their Jokes, jewels, and John Jacob Jingleheimer. They would eat Jambalaya, jellybeans, jello, play Jenga, and watch the Jungle Book.

For Christmas the home was transformed into a magic Christmas cottage. The house was decorated with wreaths, holly, angels, nutcrackers, manger scenes, blinking lights, Santas, and stars. The house smelled like Christmas, and sounded like Christmas with the festive sounds piped throughout the house the moment December first rolled around. Everything would already have been planned out, set up, hung up, wrapped up, and baked so that the Christmas month could be enjoyed in peace and serenity to fully absorb the meaning of Christmas.

Even though James was the father, a man, he managed to keep Jenny's traditions alive. With some sort of miraculous divine intervention the home looked and felt the same on each subsequent holiday after her passing. He managed this even though he never remarried, worked many hours to support his family, raised his children, was involved in their lives, fulfilled church responsibilities and community duties. Of course Jenny was sorely missed and the family always took a few moments each holiday to reflect on her life and what she meant to them, and to offer up a prayer of gratitude for her, and to verbalized a few memories.

The hour was growing late. It was now well after midnight and Jer was snoring lightly on the couch and Janet who was still curled up in the lazy boy was now fast asleep as well. Jake stood groaning as he straightened his stiff back declaring he was now heading to his old roost to catch up on lost sleep. "Goodnight Jason," he said, as he patted him on the chest yawning at the same time. Finally Jennifer stood and knelt down beside Jason resting her hands on his knees. Looking into his eyes she quietly said, "Jason, it was wonderful to have you here with the rest of the J's. It's been a long long time and it makes my heart sing." Jason looked into her kind, loving eyes and in a soft voice broken with some emotion said, "Thanks Jen, it has been a long time. I'm sorry it took dads passing to bring us all together."

Jennifer stood up and walked over to the mantle on the fireplace and grabbed an old black leather book. She handed it to Jason saying, "I found this sitting on dad's desk. It's his old black book that we always saw him writing in over the years. It's funny that none of us ever asked him what the book was, or why he wrote in it. I was only able to glance through it earlier today but thought you would be interested in looking at it." With that she turned, wrapping her robe more tightly around her pajamas, and headed upstairs to the room of her childhood.

Jason sat in the rocker with the black book in his lap. He rubbed the leather with his fingertips alternately staring into the now red embers of the once flaming fire. His mind recalled many nights his father sat at his desk writing, jotting down stuff in this book. It was funny, or as he clarified his thoughts, strange, that none of them ever did wonder to ask what the book was? Was it his journal? Was it a collection of his thoughts? Was it a list of memories? Was it just work notes and equations and scribblings of busyness? Maybe it was just grocery lists, to do items, and calendaring? Growing up it was just their dad doing whatever a dad did. Why would anyone need to ask?

Now his father was gone and here he sat in his house at Christmas time holding the black book in his lap. Now, after all these years, now he was curious what was in its pages. For some strange reason he held his breath as he opened the book and glanced down at the page before him.

The words were written in black ink and surround by an artful box. "This is my book, a collection of many different things that represent who I am, what I like, what I did, and what I thought. It's not really a journal but more of a composition that someone may be able to piece together something about me if they are interested. It's more for me to know that I was here, I lived, I experienced, I felt, I learned, and that I engaged in this life. It's lists, it's ideas, it's thoughts, it's opinions, it's things I did, things I wanted to do, and some goals, and some dreams. It's really just me smattering stuff in some pages for my later self to read and maybe smile, maybe cry, maybe laugh, maybe ponder, and maybe wonder why I wrote it in the first place. So to my future self, and anyone else if they ever do read this, enjoy."

Jason looked back into the fireplace and thought what an odd beginning to a book? He wasn't sure how to take the intro to his father's book. He wondered what his dad must have been thinking as he wrote this. It sounded as if he doubted anyone would ever be interested enough in his life to ever want to read this autobiography, if that's what it could be called, or if it really was just a book he kept, to review every so often, for self satisfaction purposes?

Nevertheless it intrigued him who this man he called father was. He moistened his fingers, turned the pages, and began reading.

The first thing he came across was a list of historical places his father had been to. It was a fairly extensive list. It started when he was a child himself and continued up until two months ago. It listed places like, the Jefferson Memorial, Mount Rushmore, Gettysburg, Arlington National Cemetery, Martins Cove, the Alamo, Acoma, Valley Forge, and the Donner Memorial. From the list he realized how much his father had appreciated the history of America and the stories that made her what she was.

He remembered how many times his father had spoken with them about love of country, patriotism, duty, and honor. He remembered how every time they sang the national anthem in church his eyes would fill with tears and his voice would crack as he sang that song barely being able to finish it. He remembered how the 4th of July was always a big to do in their house and how his dad always wore his American flag shirt and played patriotic music throughout the day. He always saluted the flag, voted, worked on campaigns, and at times ranted about how the country was going to the dogs. His father not only taught them about love of country, he showed it to them in his actions and words.

Jason kept turning the pages of the book stopping briefly at points that caught his eye. Some were simple sketches others were diagrams, some were mind maps, others were stick figures portraying ideas as if to emphasis it to the mind for remembering. One of the pages had a sketch of a ring with a heart inside of the circle. It looked like it was a depiction of his mother's wedding ring. He stopped on that page and read the words that looked as if they were written in a slow methodical hand compared with other entries of the book.

"Jenny is very, very, sick today. I do not think she will last through the night. I've been holding her in my arms for the past four hours. She looks so frail, so thin, so tired. She told me earlier she was ready to go back home. She didn't mean our home, but her heavenly home. She said she was so tired and felt so weak. Tears just rolled down my cheeks as she spoke with such an effort. She tried with all her might to raise her hand to wipe the tears from my face. With the greatest of effort she managed to capture a tear as it rolled down. Her eyes met mine and a deep sadness filled them. In a voice almost too faint to hear she told me it hurt her to see me sorrowing. She whispered how much she loved me and how much being married to me meant to her. She then named each one of our children by turn, "Jenny, Jake, Jason, Janet, Jer. Then with the greatest of exertion, and after each name, she would smile and simply say, I love her, or I love him"

Jason felt his owns eyes fill with water as he read his father's words. In his heart he was imagining his father's heart breaking. What must it have been like for him to hold his mother in her last few hours of life? What must have the weight been like to know your wife will be gone and you have four little people at home thinking mom will be home any day now and that life would just continue on as it always had.

He rested the black book on his chest and stared once again into the fire. He felt the weight of the memory upon his heart. As a child he had seen only his perspective and had entirely missed his father's experience. After a brief reflection he opened the book again and randomly flipped to another page.

"Jason and I went fishing today for his first time. What a hoot that was. I think we had the fishing line in more trees and bushes than in the water. At least, I had my line in more trees and bushes. Ha-ha. Jason seemed to be a natural at it! Here I thought I would take him up and teach Him all my collective knowledge, which truth be told, would only take a minute or so, but he taught me much more through his actions. He just took to it. His casting was great, and he even caught three rainbows where I never caught a single one. What a time we had."

A smile crossed Jason's face as he clearly remembered that day. It was a beautiful June morning on a mountain lake not far from their home. He was so excited to go fishing. He remembered well each fish he had reeled in, the thrill of the bite, the fight on the reel, and his dad netting them. He even remembered how good they tasted when they cooked them that night for family dinner. It was just he and his dad. He never even paused to wonder why his brothers or sisters had not come along. It never occurred to him that it was just Jason and dad time. He looked into the fire again and realized his father must have done that with his other siblings as well, and he never realized that either.

Thumbing through the black book again he came across another list. He was amazed at all the lists his father had made. They didn't have any commentary or thoughts along with the lists, just bullets. But compiled and analyzed, a person could glean much about this man and what was important in his life.

This list was his top five and then his top ten favorite books. Looking at the books they were all classics like, Ben Hur - The Tale of the Christ, David Copperfield, The Odyssey, Les Miserable, and others. Some of them he had read several times. What was funny, if a book belonged to a set, and he really liked the books in the set, he counted it as one book so he could evidently include it in his top five or top ten and still call it his top five or ten.

He had remembered his dad talking about some of these books at the kitchen table, but he had never really been interested or gave it much thought. His father appeared to have been a well read man, something he really never associated with his dad. How could he have missed that?

Now he was fascinated with the black book. He sat in the chair by the fireplace reading until the glowing embers began to fade. He went back to the beginning and turned page after page reading, absorbing, and feeling the hand written ink on the white lined pages of the book. He sat there amazed at times, crying at times, laughing at times, remembering at times, and pondering in between them all. It appeared to him that his father understood that life was a limited proposition and that making the most of it as often as one could was important.

Yet viewing his father's life he also realized it's not a daily storybook where the knight on the gallant white charger saves the day. He had sorrows and trials and disappointments. Fear and anxiety played their parts as well. Life was a buffet of, well, life. As Shakespeare had written, "All the world's a stage, and all the men and women merely players: they have their exits and their entrances; and one man in his time plays many parts..." And on that stage are all of life's vicissitudes, triumphs, endurances, and many days of sameness.

His father, to Jason, growing up, just seemed to handle whatever it was, and was just a dad, and did what dads are expected to do. He never thought of him as cultured, interesting, experienced, or whatever adjectives he accredited to other men at school or on television, in the news or wherever. Now he found him simple, yet complex, intelligent yet understanding, hard working yet fun, dutiful, yet kind. He had misjudged his father all because he never bothered to look deeper into his life or try to understand him or be involved more in his life of his own accord. Dad was a fixture like a lamp stand, very useful when you needed light to see by, but the rest of the time collected dust.

Now that he was gone, now he was coming to understand him, now it was too late. Maybe it was the Christmas season, maybe it was being back in his childhood home, maybe it was being with his siblings, or maybe it was a quiet spirit whispering to him as he sat by the smoldering fire. With the Christmas lights illuminating the room, he earnestly tried to understand who his father really was. His hurting heart began to soften. Whatever it was he felt, it was as if he had been sitting in a dark room and someone had just turned on the light.

Reading through the book Jason came across the time when he had decided to leave home and seek a life different from the one he had been raised in with his family, his family being deeply religious. Their faith was a defining part of who they were, how they viewed life, and how they identified themselves. Jason remembered well the night he told his father how he didn't want to live their religion anymore and how it held him back from everything he enjoyed. That it was too restrictive and archaic. He had taken up addictive habits and stopped attending Sunday services. He knew his father would be disappointed but that too was something he didn't want to feel pushed down by. He left, and made his way in life pretty much forgetting his family. Years past and now he was reliving that experience, in the same room where he had told his father he was leaving, only now through words written on a page.

His father had written of that experience, "Talked with Jas tonight. My heart is heavy and I'm filled with sorrow. Not sure how to console my heart. All I know is it burns like a fire consuming my emotions. I feel as if a part of me has died. I want to simply slump on floor and cry. I know he has hurts and sorrows that I cannot fix. I know he has chosen a road that will bring more sadness in his life. I wanted so much more for him. I wish he would remember Jesus Christ, the little child born in Bethlehem, the Christ who healed and loved the people, the Savior of the world who bled in the garden, died on the cross and left the tomb empty. If only he would understand that it is He who can heal all wounds, strengthen our weaknesses and insecurities, give us hope when our faith is weak, and lift us when we fall or are unsure. If Jason were here again, I'd tell him to put his trust in the only sure thing, Jesus Christ, the Son of God, and to hold on and move forward until he has enough faith and hope on his own to sustain himself. I love him with all my heart and soul and can only hope someday he will come to himself and return."

Jason sat there in silence. He had left the spirit long ago; yet sitting in this home where the spirit was present melted away his rebellious exterior. He couldn't conjure up the words he felt as he read that entry. His life, his decisions, had carried him to unexpected places and experiences. He had experienced sorrows and disappointments that at times were overwhelming. He had felt alone through many of them. His first marriage had been a disaster, as the one after that had been. His friends were shallow and fair weathered, his health was suffering due to his addictive habits, and what had he gained? For a moment he allowed his mind to ponder the question, "What if?" What if he had kept his faith in Christ? What if he had embraced his family and had kept in touch with them and been apart of their lives? What if he had not rebelled and started habits that now seemed impossible to break? "Yes," he thought, "What if, indeed."

The black book had given Jason an insight into his father he had never known. He saw into his mind and into his heart. He had relived his experiences and accomplishments. He stood up and laid the book on the mantle of the fireplace. The fire within was now extinguished and the glowing embers had gone black. Resting both hands on the mantle he looked up at the picture above the fireplace where hung a family portrait done the year his mother had passed away. Both his parents were now gone, the funeral was in two days for his father, the wheel of time had turned, and it wasn't going to turn backwards.

What was this thing called family? Was it more than just a bunch of humans congregating in a group? Was there more of a connection? Was it more than just a mortal entity to facilitate birthing and raising children? Or was it, as his father had always said, "an eternal unit meant to withstand the tests of mortality and enjoy the eternities together in peace, love, and joy?" If it was, he had fallen out of the wagon and needed to decide if he wanted to climb back in and be a part of this great experience.

Christmas was three days away. He would have time to think and ponder and review and decide if he wanted to make any course corrections. All he knew now was that his mother was a saint and he loved and respected her and her passing had sent him into a tailspin. His father was a man who he posthumously had gotten to know and loved him more than he previously knew. Christmas was a time of Christ. It is a time of remembering Him and what a better time to heal and change than at the season where we remember the Savior even more. He remembered the words of scripture his father use to quote, "If ye have felt the song of redeeming love, can you feel so now?" He felt his heart could hear that song faintly in the background.

It was time to change. As his father had always said, "Its never to late to change so long as the Master says there is still time." He knew it would require a change of heart, but he also knew Christ can change hearts if we open it up to Him.

The Gift

Elizabeth Mansfield had wanted to be a mom for as long as she could remember. Even as a little girl her favorite toys to play with were baby dolls. Especially the one she had gotten for her seventh birthday, the one that she could feed with a bottle and moments later a diaper would need to be changed.

Even when she was fourteen she loved baby-sitting, in fact, she was in high demand by all the parents in her neighborhood. The children loved her and their parents knew it. It wasn't that her games were any better, or that she was more fun, or even trusted more by moms and dads, but it was a genuine love everyone could feel emanate from her. It was hard to describe but anyone who was around her could somehow feel the power that love resonated.

It was surprising then that Elizabeth never got married. Somehow the years slipped by and the wedding bells never rang.

Elizabeth dunked another snicker doodle in her steaming cup of hot chocolate as she sat in her kitchen reading one of the children's Christmas books she had just rented from the library. Turning the last page of the book she glanced at her watch, it was time to go. Finishing the last sip of her hot chocolate she stuffed the books into her backpack and walked to the front room grabbing her warm jacket from the coat rack and stepped out the door of her cozy apartment.

Braving the chill of December's night air Elizabeth walked briskly to the bus stop pausing several times to adjust the scarf which covered her nose and mouth. She was grateful, especially tonight, that the city had finally installed the new lit bus shelters they had been promising for years. As she waited in the glass enclosure of the stop for the sixth street bus, Elizabeth briskly rubbed her gloved hands together giving them that little extra bit of warmth that kept them comfortable.

Elizabeth stared through the glass of the bus shelter into the clear star-filled sky and wondered if anyone up there really was aware of whom we were or the deeds we did? "With so many stars," she thought, "there must be an awful lot of people in that universe, and with so many people in that big universe, who would ever notice a small insignificant child?" Her thoughts led her to the thought that maybe that was why so many of them suffered in the world.

The crackling of the ice and snow beneath the wheels of the approaching bus brought her back to reality. She watched as the bus came to a complete stop in front of her and stared up as the doors opened outward revealing a set of stairs and a smiling bus driver. "Evenin' Miss Elizabeth," came the words from the smiling driver. "Goin to St. Luke's again tonight?"

"Yes Charles," came the reply, "I have some little friends I need to cheer up." "Yes indeed Miss Elizabeth, especially during the Christmas season I'd imagine." The doors of the bus closed preventing the icy air from continuing to flow inside. Charles put the bus into gear and giving it gas pulled away from the curb into the night.

The glow of the lights from inside the bus illuminated the passengers as they made their way along sixth street picking up more evening travelers heading to their Christmas Eve traditions. At each stop riders laden with Christmas presents and yuletide gifts shuffled on and rushed off the bus in a hurry to reach their destinations of celebration.

As the bus paused at a traffic light next to the local church a choir could be heard singing "Once in Royal David's City" to the passersby. Elizabeth looked out the window of the bus admiring the sweet sound of the Christmas carol and became transfixed on the manger scene which was set up outside. She looked at the baby Jesus in his cradle and thought about his birth. She marveled at how the birth of one baby two thousand years ago was able to change a world. She thought about the new star that had appeared introducing this advent and of heavenly beings that had appeared to shepherds telling them about peace on earth and goodwill to men.

The roar of the bus moving forward brought Elizabeth back to reality once more. As the bus continued to make its way to St Luke's she pondered on what it must have been like to know this Jesus when he was a child. There was no record of that period of his life except that he "learned and grew in wisdom and stature."

Yet she thought he must have been a very thoughtful and kind child. Sober, yet joyful. He must have brought great joy to his earthly parents as well as his heavenly parents. For how could it have been otherwise seeing how his adult life was filled with amazing acts of compassion and charity? She thought about the verses in the Bible in which Jesus told his disciples to, "suffer the little children to come unto me, for of such is the kingdom of God." "Yes," she whispered, with a smile, "he had to be aware of each precious little child." Yet her heart still struggled with why so many had to suffer so much?

The bus sped on through the cold December night revealing house after house ornamented with the decorations of the season giving variety to a neighborhood usually drab at this time of the evening. The bus pulled into the parking lot in front of St Luke's hospital. Elizabeth stood up from her seat grabbing her bag and walked to the front of the bus where the door was open waiting for its occupants to exit. Touching Charles, the bus driver, on the shoulder she wished him a Merry Christmas. Charles returned the holiday wish and admiringly watched her step off of the bus.

The doors closed and Elizabeth heard the bus roar off into the wintry night as she walked to the entrance of the facility. The glass sliding doors opened revealing an empty lobby aglow with fluorescent lights and a huge Christmas tree.

"Good evening Miss Mansfield," echoed the voice, from behind the information desk.

"Good evening Amanda," Elizabeth replied, offering a warm smile along with the greeting. "How is Alfred feeling?"

"He is much better, thank you. He asked me to thank you for the cookies you brought yesterday, they lifted his spirits."

Elizabeth continued, "Tell him we hope his leg heals quickly and to be more careful on those icy steps next time. They're so dangerous in the winter." She patted Amanda on the hand offering a smile once again before turning and walking towards the elevator.

Elizabeth pushed the call button for the up elevator. Within a few minutes the doors opened and she stepped inside. The Christmas music, which was piped into the elevator, was peaceful and calm. She pushed the illuminated number five-button and watched as the doors closed lifting the elevator upwards. As Elizabeth rode the elevator to the fifth floor of the tall building she once again drifted into her own thoughts.

She knew that each person eventually had to pass from this life of mortality to a world beyond the grave. No one got out of that. Yet, deep inside, she wondered why little children had to die. It saddened her heart each time she would think about it. "They had their whole lives in front of them," she whispered to herself, with a trace of anguish in her voice, "there is so much for them to learn, to experience, to be a part of; education, family, relationships, adventure, and years of happy productive lives should be theirs. Why couldn't they live to grow up? Why couldn't they experience the joys of life? Why did they have to endure so much pain and suffering? It just doesn't seem fair."

The beep of the elevator signaled that the fifth floor had come. The doors slid open and Elizabeth stepped off onto the pediatric oncology floor of the hospital. Here is where the hardest hearts became softened butter. It was difficult to look into the faces of these fragile little children and not have compassion for their suffering.

They came here from all over the region. Parents with children diagnosed with terminal illnesses looking for a miracle. Some found that miracle; most did not, and left with tears and a void in their lives. Yet it was here that they had the best opportunity, at least the best medical opportunity, for a cure.

Some children however, were saved, not because of the advanced medical treatments but because it truly was a miracle, something medicine had no explanations for. Yet everyone that came was looking for a miracle, to be that one special case, the exception to the rule, that miracle.

The Gift

It was here that Elizabeth came most evenings after she had already worked a full day cleaning everyone's teeth at the dentist's office. She came to lift the sad countenances, inspire hope in little hearts, create courage for the soul, wipe away tears of fear and pain from small eyes, and touch lives with love.

It was here that Elizabeth found life, her life. An interesting phenomenon she would often think, finding life where there was death. Yet somehow she felt it was the most important work she could do, to hold on to a little pair of hands tightly in hers as she helped them make the transition from here to there. Here being a world of suffering and there being a world of rest.

Elizabeth couldn't count how many times she had held the hand of a child as they made this final journey, but she knew it was many. She had been making the bus ride to St Luke's for over ten years.

Most of the time parents of the failing children were there. But many times, by default, she happened to be the one who was there in the final minutes of life. It would usually be very quiet in the room except for the ticking of machines and the strained breathing of the patient. Darkness filled the room. She would open a book with wonderfully large pictures and read the words softly to the heavy breathing of a child. Most at this stage did not see the pictures, and the words of her voice drifted into their ears as if through a tunnel miles long.

Yet Elizabeth found joy in volunteering, to just be a friend, play games, read stories, laugh, and give hugs. She was anxiously awaited by the children of the fifth floor as well as by the staff of doctors and nurses.

Elizabeth walked to the nurse's station to inform the head nurse on the evening shift that she had arrived. "How is Gabrielle tonight," she asked, hoping for a positive answer. "Not well," came the unwanted reply. "She is very weak and has been sleeping most of the day." Elizabeth sighed as her hand covered her heart. "Is it okay to go in and see her?" The reply was affirmative and Elizabeth made her way to room 5683. As she reached the door a wave of emotion began to overtake her and she fumbled in her bag for a tissue.

Pausing in front of the door trying to build her courage, to not show any sign of sadness, Elizabeth reflected on how this child had had such an impact on her, more than all of the other children. Even though all of the other ones had been special.

Gabrielle had been abandoned when she was born. Her mother, whoever she was, had given her life only to drop her off at the doors of a local police station.

She had been in five foster homes in her short seven and a half year life. Each home she had been in was able to experience her exuberant and happy disposition. All of them were glad they were given the opportunity to know her. Each felt their lives had been added to by having her life touch theirs.

Yet a trail of tragedy always followed her. Each time it looked as if one of the families might adopt her, trouble always seemed to strike the family. Sometimes financial, sometimes sickness, and other times internal strife.

The last family she had stayed with, the Sorenson's were the ones to discover her sickness. They had severe financial difficulties and were forced to move to another state. Gabrielle had complained about severe pain and was taken to several medical doctors where they diagnosed her terminal condition. As a ward of the state her hospital and medical expenses were covered, but the sad circumstance was that she had to face this terrible trial alone.

Oh sure there were people who took her to her treatments, fetched her medicines, gave her a room to sleep in, and food to eat, but no one who personally cared for her, no one whom she felt truly loved her and who would miss her when she was gone, no one except Elizabeth Mansfield.

Gabrielle and Elizabeth were kindred spirits. Even though there were forty years between them, there was a bond, a deep friendship that fused the two together. Even though they had only known each other for a short time, less than three months, they both felt their relationship had existed from a time long before this sphere of existence.

The Gift

It was remarkable how much alike they were. They would both laugh at the same things. They were interested in the same books, liked the same foods, shared the same fondness for Christmas, and both their favorite colors were blue. They could almost read one another's thoughts and feelings. Elizabeth was like the mother Gabrielle never had and Gabrielle was as the daughter Elizabeth never had. If some one were to look upon them, they would vow the two were family. Yet they were not.

It was this unusual bond that made this passing of a child such a heartbreaking matter for Elizabeth. She felt as if her entire being would melt into oblivion. She did not know how she would be able to help her little Gabrielle make her final journey. It was almost too hard to bear.

If only they could have met years ago. If only she could have been a mother to this little girl, to kiss her forehead goodnight, to bandage up her scraped knees, to celebrate her first part in a play, to wipe away her tears of sadness, to cuddle up in a big pillow-covered bed and read stories together. Alas it was not meant to be. She had lived her life of loneliness, and Gabrielle had lived hers, and by some divine chance both ships happened to pass in the night. Now was the time that had been given to them.

What a special time these short three months had been for them both. A unity and friendship had been forged which would pass the veil of mortality and time and would bind them together. It was a love that would reach through the eternities.

As Elizabeth stared at the door of Gabrielle's room she silently prayed for strength, the strength to see Gabrielle in the final moments of her life, the strength to smile and show confidence, the strength to send her back home into the arms of a loving Heavenly Father who was waiting for her return. She wiped the torrent of tears from her eyes, and composing herself, opened the door.

She stepped into the silent room. A small Winnie-the-Pooh night light created a glow in the darkened room. Elizabeth quietly shut the large door to the room. Softly she walked over to the side of the hospital bed where Gabrielle lay. She stared down into her gentle face. With all of the tubes, monitors, and IV's that invaded her body she marveled that she looked so peaceful.

71

Elizabeth reached down and stroked her smooth face with her fingers. She traced the outline of her precious little face, and caressed the dainty features of her eyes, her tiny nose, and rosy cheeks. She stroked her hair again and again finally bending over to kiss her forehead. Tears from her eyes ran down the auburn hair of Gabrielle and soaked the pillow, which braced her head.

Gabrielle's eyes opened. She had felt the presence of Elizabeth. Her weary eyes looked up and caught the view of a river of tears flowing from Elizabeth. She lifted her feeble hand and touched Elizabeth on the cheek. Elizabeth felt the fragile hand and brought her hand to cover that of Gabrielle's. "Don't cry," came the soft quivering voice of Gabrielle. "It will be okay. I get to go home tonight." Elizabeth moved Gabrielle's hand to her lips so she could kiss the palm. Elizabeth held Gabrielle's hand tightly to her lips. After a moment Elizabeth looked Gabrielle in her eyes and gently stroking her hair said, "How do you know."

Gabrielle's strained and tired voice responded, "An angel came a little while ago and told me that Jesus was waiting for me and that it was time to go." She paused a moment to catch her breath and continued, "He told me to be happy, that many people who loved me were also waiting for me and all we had to do was open the door and we would be there."

Elizabeth held onto one of Gabrielle's hands and squeezed tightly while tenderly touching her cheek with the other. "But," Gabrielle continued, after once again catching her breath, "I told him I couldn't go until you came to say good-bye. I told him I couldn't go until I told you how much I loved you." Gabrielle lifted her other hand all burdened with tubes and tape and put it around Elizabeth's neck. Elizabeth bent down hugging her as best as she could with all of the monitoring equipment. The words, "I love you so much," penetrated Elizabeth's ears like the warmth of the sun penetrates a snow-covered meadow.

Elizabeth reached out her hand once again touching Gabrielle's face and said, "I love you too Gabrielle, you are the joy of my life. Oh how I will miss you. Oh how I will miss you so very, very much." A feeling of warmth and love pervaded both of them like a warm summer breeze blowing through tall green grass rustling the tender blades together.

"I brought you a Christmas present," whispered Elizabeth. Gabrielle looked at her with excitement and wonder. For the moment she forgot that the angel was waiting for her. "A present," she responded, with delicate joy. "What did you bring me?" Elizabeth reached into her bag and pulled out the most precious doll Gabrielle had ever seen. She held the doll close to Gabrielle so she could reach it. With both her weak hands Gabrielle took the doll and held it close to her heart. "It's lovely," she said, "what should I name her?" "Anything you like dear," replied Elizabeth. "I think I will name her Gabrielle."

Elizabeth looked at her somewhat puzzled and asked, "Why do you want to name her Gabrielle?" "Because," she answered, stroking the hair of the doll, "it will help you remember me when I go. I don't want you to ever forget me," said Gabrielle, as tears began to fill her eyes. She repeated the words again while hugging the doll, "I don't want you to ever forget me." Elizabeth hugged Gabrielle tightly and whispered in her ear, "Child, I could never forget you, I will always be thinking of you till I make the same journey."

"Now, shall I read you my favorite Christmas story?" Elizabeth offered, drying her eyes. "Yes, I would like that," answered Gabrielle. Elizabeth opened the pages to the large picture book and began reading the words, pausing after each page to show Gabrielle the beautifully illustrated pictures that accompanied the story. As she read each page Gabrielle's breathing became heavier and heavier. As Elizabeth was showing her another picture she noticed her breathing became very still and a calm peacefulness over came her. Holding up the Christmas book Elizabeth heard the final breath of Gabrielle escape from her lips. A sweet smile graced her delicate face.

Elizabeth slowly closed the book and laid it on the bed. She grabbed Gabrielle's hand and held it to her face and cried. Oh how she would miss this precious little princess. She kissed her hand and gently placed it on the bed. Leaning over the lifeless body Elizabeth kissed her forehead one last time and sat down beside the bed in the dark room with only the glow of the night-light to illuminate the passing of another child.

As Elizabeth sat quietly next to the still body of Gabrielle tears began to flow again. She bowed her head into her hands and sobbed. The flood of tears flowing from her eyes was the breaking of the dam of all the sorrows she had experienced for all the children who had passed away over the last ten years. She sat for a while quietly in the room next to the body, which had housed the spirit of Gabrielle.

Elizabeth finally stood, wiping her nose and eyes with her handkerchief and looked down on the bed where the doll was tucked under one arm of Gabrielle. She tenderly lifted her arm and removed the doll. She held it close to her chest for a moment reflecting on what had happened. She wasn't sad for Gabrielle any more. Her suffering had ended. Elizabeth was sad now not because of her sufferings but because she would miss her.

Elizabeth walked to the door of the room and slowly opened it exposing the well-lit hallway of the fifth floor. She walked to the nurse's station to inform them Gabrielle had passed away. With compassion in her voice the head nurse held Elizabeth's hand and said, "We know. Will you be alright?" Elizabeth looked into her eyes and replied, "Yes, I will, Merry Christmas."

She rode the elevator to the first floor. Walking across the lobby she paused a moment at the great Christmas tree. She stared at its lights and the presents beneath the tree, and then to the doll in her hands. She had brought the gift to a dying little girl who couldn't take it with her who in return, gave the gift back with more meaning. Elizabeth held the doll out in front of her and stared at it with the reflection of the Christmas lights illuminating its face. She smiled realizing how much it actually looked like Gabrielle. She kissed the doll and walked out into the cold night.

Somehow the chill in the December air didn't seem quite as cold as when she came. She didn't notice the bus when it pulled up in front of her. Looking up she saw the smile of Charles greeting her. He didn't say a word, just offered her a warm smile. Stepping onto the bus she returned the smile and sat down.

The Gift

She admired the houses with all their decorations as she rode the illuminated bus home. Opening the door to her apartment she walked in. Glancing around the quiet room she was grateful for the privilege of being there when another precious child passed on. Even more she was grateful for the blessing of knowing Gabrielle. It truly was a wonder this journey called death.

She placed Gabrielle, the doll, on the sofa in front of the Christmas tree and after pouring a cup of hot chocolate sprinkled with mini marshmallows sat down next to the doll and watched the flickering of the flames in the gas fireplace. Her heart felt heavy and sorrow settled over her soul. She sipped the soothing drink enjoying the warmth it gave to her hands.

Just as she was about to drift off to sleep she noticed a light begin to fill the room. It started small and faint almost as if a part of the flames of the fire. The light increased in size and intensity until it filled the corner of the room next to where Elizabeth was sitting. She looked into the brightness and noticed the outline of a figure standing as it were in the middle of the light. Within moments the figure came into full view. There in the corner of the room, dressed in exquisite white, looking beautiful and happy stood Gabrielle.

Elizabeth stared in awe at the vision. Holding her breath she raised her hands to her lips afraid to speak. Gabrielle walked to the edge of the sofa where Elizabeth sat and knelt on the floor beside her and spoke in a sweet, almost angelic voice and said, "I am fine Elizabeth, please do not be sad for me, I am very happy, thank you for being there when I had to go. I will be here for you when you come." Elizabeth watched as Gabrielle stood and smiled a big warm smile and turned and walked through a tunnel seemingly made of the whitest light she had ever seen.

After watching the light disappear, a joy that was indescribable filled her entire being. She realized that all of us have our time here in mortality, some quite lengthy and others very short. Yet our time, our existence was a unique experience for each of us. She understood that each person experiences suffering as a part of this realm as well as joy and happiness. In the end each of us has a place of peace in some degree according to what we did here.

Elizabeth knew the peace she felt at this moment was because of the time and love she gave to a little girl who had no one.

She reflected for a small moment on all she had experienced and felt this Christmas Eve and realized that this was what Christmas was all about. It is about love, service, and giving of oneself to someone else.

Elizabeth stood up and looked at the small manger scene on her end table and thought that every one of us was in the hands of that babe born in a manger two thousand years ago. He was aware of us all. He took upon him all of our sorrows, grief, and sufferings. He truly did know how to succor each child who suffered.

She smiled as she walked off to her bedroom. Tomorrow would bring a new day and quite possibly another child who would be grateful because there truly was someone in the world who cared.

The Return

Andrew exhaled the now warm air from his lungs and watched as that warm air penetrated through the surrounding cold and crisp air like a puff of smoke from a fireplace. The breath of air dissipated quickly as it rose upwards into the night sky. Snowflakes drifted slowly to earth from the heavens and piled one on top of the other. Millions of them had accumulated and began sticking together eventually creating the now two feet deep pile of snow that graced the front yard.

Each flake fell effortlessly straight down with only a slight side to side motion from the resistance of the surrounding air. There was no wind tonight, and a full moon blanketed the entire neighborhood in a very faint yellowish hue. It could be seen just over the mountains to the east between the clouds that were unloading their cargo of frozen water.

It was Christmas. The traditional Christmas Eve celebrations were now over. The old grandfather clock had chimed its twelve chimes indicating that the eve of Christmas had past and ahead lay Christmas Day. The children had all gone to bed, or at least were asleep in assorted places throughout the house. Some had fallen asleep on the sofa by the fireplace; others on the floor by the grand Christmas tree and the remainder were tucked between goose down comforters on mom and dad's bed. Somehow these rooms seemed to preserve the Christmas feeling better than their own beds in their own rooms.

The Christmas Eve celebration earlier had been one to remember. The beautifully symmetrical Spruce tree filled the air with the scent of pine and had been decorated with popcorn garlands, nuts, fruits, candles, and home made ornaments made from brown paper bags, glue, glitter, and string. Under that wonderful homemade tree were presents wrapped in colorful paper with little labels identifying the recipients of the homemade gifts that were hidden inside.

This Christmas was the year they had all decided to retreat from all of the commercialization the season had evolved into and make the Christmas celebration simpler, and more filled with the spirit of what the season truly is about, and that is a celebration of the Savior of the world. Angela,

Andrew's wife, had thought of the idea and had presented it to the family with mixed responses at first, and then the excitement began to grow as each person become involved and put their heart into it.

Sweet songs had filled the air and wafted on angel's wings through out the house and through the walls into the chilly air of the night. Food filled the red and green decorated kitchen table. There was rich hot chocolate with tiny marshmallows floating on top, spicy hot apple cider with cinnamon sticks, creamy eggnog, red and white spiraled candy canes, dark nut filled chocolates, multiple varieties of cheeses, black forest ham, and tiny pieces of pumpernickel bread all laid out for easy reach by everyone.

Christmas cheer was exchanged by one and all to one and all. The Christmas story was read and reflected on and love and togetherness filled in the remaining voids. All in all it was one of the finest Christmas Eve's ever! Well, every Christmas seemed to be the finest ever but this one seemed more so. Everyone agreed it was probably a return to a more simple and pure celebration of the holiday that made the feeling so strong.

Yet as Andrew stood in the dark wintery front yard all was not well. It had been his tradition for many years now to come out into the Christmas Eve night and simply reflect on all that was important to him. Important things like family, the Christ child, the meaning of the season, his life, and what the coming years would bring. He enjoyed the crisp air on his face and the quietness of the late hour. He especially thought it a blessing when he could see the moon and a greater blessing if the stars joined in for a concert of light. Tonight though, he would take the moon and the falling snow.

His thoughts and remembrances tonight were on a little boy who had enjoyed these celebrations with him and his family over the previous years. He was a bright eyed, happy, adventurous little boy. He loved to play, and read, and just be around his family. In the summer months he sought adventure with his siblings in a backyard full of dirt and weeds and a clubhouse on stilts. With imaginations as big as the sun they filled the hours with countless conquests, explorations, and discoveries.

Their home school time was filled with reading good books, battling with math, passing of scouting requirements, and doing observations. The piano was played, reports were written, and questions were asked. His little life was filled with such things dreams are made of.

The years passed, as they always seem to do, and this little boy grew up. His voice deepened, he began to shave, and a desire to expand his world began. The desire to question authority, especially that of his parents, the need to place more emphasis and credibility on his friends, the need to push the boundaries on rules, and in some cases break through those boundaries. The faith he had been taught and grew up with became the cage which held him back from the greater adventures which lay out there somewhere, all around him.

Each passing month brought a little more distance between him and those who loved him. Soon, the frustrations of living within a prescribed boundary became stifling and outbursts and arguments would happen. His intelligence level had now, in his late teens, surpassed that of Andrew and Angela's. He now knew his parent knew nothing. They were simpletons who dawned the clothing and mannerisms from the puritan age. They were out of touch, out of time, and out of reality.

So as a person gains infinite knowledge, or so they think, everyone else around them become a frustration. They become the enemy who is holding them back. They don't understand. They don't see your friends as you know them, they don't understand the need to experiment with illicit substances, they don't understand the destructive behavior you, as a now mature teen, are engaging in . . . or do they?

This was the life of Loren, Andrew's son when he finally had had enough of the strict rules, the overbearing religion that wanted to control his entire life, the constant nagging, and the overwhelming questions of, "Where have you been?" "Where are you going?" What are you doing?" "Whom are you going with?" "What time will you be back?" These were questions of love and concern. These were questions that a mature mind would understand are what relationships are made of.

Loren had packed his belongings and threw them into his friend's old beater buggy and had moved out of the oppressive home where people had loved him. He was off on another grand adventure. One where he could be himself, he could define his own rules, he could make his own destructive decisions if he wanted to and no one would be able to preach to him.

He had left in a spirit of anger and frustration. He left no forwarding address, no way for anyone from his past to contact him in the present, and no desire to hear from them in the future. If his religion had taught him to pray to a loving Heavenly Father then he swept that belief under a rug. If it taught him to avoid alcohol, then he filled his glass with ale and gave a toast to freedom. If he was taught to worship God on Sundays and keep the day holy, then he found every unholy thing to occupy his time on that day.

Loren now felt free! He was the master of his own ship; he set his own sails, and found his own wind and sailed to wherever he wanted. There was now no limit on what he could do. It was wonderful what throwing away all rules and commandments could do for a person. No more inhibitions, no more shackles to bind desires, no more bridles on passions, no more feeling guilty, no more lectures, and no more wasted time following some superstitious belief in a divine personage who existed in the heavens somewhere.

With no more restraints to govern Loren's actions he lived the life of a rock star. Go where he wanted, see what he wanted, taste what he wanted, experience what he wanted, indulge in what he wanted. It was glorious! He looked back on his siblings with contempt and couldn't figure out why they closed their minds to the big universe that shone out in front of them. Why would they want to follow some cloistered life in a rigid set of stupid rules? He was convinced they had no idea what they were missing.

And so his life went on from one pile of pleasure and carefreeness to another. At times the days just seemed to run together. The pages of the calendar kept getting ripped off exposing yet another month. The year markings on those calendars kept adding another digit. Loren moved from one addiction of supposed happiness to another addiction of supposed freedom.

Each new adventure into non-responsibility and indulgence forged another link onto the chains that bound him to his profligate life. His spiritual eyes had been blinded, his spiritual ears had been deafened, and the spiritual part of his mind sealed off to the reality of God and His goodness and mercy.

He had become the product of unrestrained indulgences in a carnal and unfeeling world. What he had thought was freedom, were really hard, rough chains. What he thought was liberation was bondage, what he had thought was adventure, was really physical, spiritual, and emotional injury. His life had become dull, dirty, and deplorable.

This Christmas Eve Loren found himself sitting on an old wooden bench in a lonely park on a snowy night staring up at the little white flakes as they fell to the earth. He had no friends and no family to celebrate the season with. He was cold, yet somehow he did not mind the stinging sensation on his skin. Shivers spread around his entire body as he watched those little flakes. His mind was transported to another time and another place, where as a child, he had looked out of his upstairs bedroom window, and saw his father standing out in the snowy night of a Christmas Eve. The yellowish hue of the moonlight had cast a soft glow upon him. He was staring up at the night sky watching each tiny flake fall earthward.

He remembered it was something his father had done every Christmas Eve for as long as he could remember. Once he had asked his father why he stood out in the yard late at night every Christmas Eve? His father had told him that he liked the freshness of the winter air, and that the moon and the stars seemed to glow in such a way as to give him a glimpse into eternity. He said he used that time to think of a loving God, who loved His children, and who had sent a Savior, to save himself, Loren, the family, and all mankind from sin and death. It was his way of reflecting deeply on his life, what he had done, where he was, and what he should do better.

As Loren's mind reflected on this memory he realized he had tears rolling down his cheeks. It surprised him. From somewhere deep beneath the crust he had built around his heart these little liquid manifestations had seeped through. Subconsciously he had used that same moment to reflect on his own life, on what he had done, and what he had become, and he found that he came up short. He had not found liberation and freedom from oppressive rules and ridiculous religious requirements, but he had found sadness, depression, and deceit, in the promises of a world that promoted life without a divine Father who looks down from the heavens upon us all.

His decisions had brought him to exactly where he was, sitting on a bench with no family to hug and love him, no friends who were tried and true, and no meaning or purpose to life except just another day. His consequences for the decisions made were addictions to drink, drugs, and degrading habits. He was ill, tired, and defeated. How he wished he could turn back the hands of time, reattach those calendar months that fleeted by. He would change one moment in time if that gift were given him. That moment would be the decision to leave a loving family in search of stupidity.

All the wishing in the world could not do that. He was not a fictional character in a magical book that somehow wakes up to realize he had been dreaming all along and that everything was okay. He was worn down and sick sitting on a cold bench, on a cold night, surrounded by a cold world, feeling like life was ebbing out of him.

As each snowflake continued to fall to the earth he wished even more to be in the loving arms of that father who pondered about the good and the joys life had to offer. How he wished he had not left the faith that had made his father such a great man. How he wished he had had the vision to follow the footsteps of the Master teacher, the Savior of the world, the Prince of peace. Why had the offerings of the world looked so enticing to him? Why had the empty promises seemed so full of opportunity? Why was it so important to experience a beverage filled with alcohol that dulled the senses and took away ones control and freedom? Why had it been so important to ingest chemicals that altered the way one thought? Why would a person turn over control of their will to a substance that neither cares nor respects? Why was it so important to use foul language to impress others when all it did was to amplify ignorance? Why was it so important to sweep God under a rug when it is the love of God that gives life meaning? Why had he viewed the commandments from a loving Heavenly

Father as oppressive and restrictive, when in reality they were liberating and progressive? Why, why, why?

The questions just kept multiplying in his mind until he lay in a heap on the ground next to the old wooden bench, snow piling on top of him. Loren's life had been a paradox. He was brought up in a good home, with good parents, who taught good things. He had been taught to have faith, hope, and to be kind and serve other people. He had experienced what it was like to have true joy by living the kind of life God had intended His children to live.

Yet with that knowledge, he still chose the opposite experience, experiences that did not bring peace, nor joy, and no contentment. It was precisely the kind of life he had chosen that had left him feeling hopeless, afraid, resentful, and suspicious of the motives of others. He had found the exact opposite of what he thought he was getting. He had become a victim of the big lie!

As Andrew stood in the chill air reflecting on that little boy, he wondered where that little boy was? What was he doing? Was he all right? Did he miss his family? What could they have done better? Would he ever see that bright eyed, happy faced little boy again? With all his joy over his family, their goodness and faithfulness, he still sorrowed over his lost sheep, his prodigal son.

He couldn't explain it, but somehow a parent's love for their child was stronger than time, stronger than space, and stronger than the devils laughter. His prayers that night penetrated the clouds and passed by the moon and stars and found their way to the ears of a loving Father who lives in the heavens. The prayer of that faithful father standing in a snow covered yard brought down the powers of heaven upon a little boy who had now grown up into a lost and wayward young man with no hope.

As Loren lay in the park, snow covering his body, he felt the hands of death touching his heart. Somehow he wanted to stir himself, rise up one more time, but the energy, the hope, the desire, was gone. There was nothing within him to chase away those cold hands that were now embracing him even tighter.

Through his eyes he thought he saw two worlds, one world was the snow filled park where he lay, and the other an ethereal world with many voices and blurring images of people moving about. He felt as if he needed to go toward the ethereal world he saw. Suddenly, there appeared tingling shafts of light that seemed to dart in and out of his body. The light, and the warmth from the light, invigorated him. He felt an over whelming feeling of love envelope him in such a way that he felt immersed in this feeling. It was beyond any description.

He came to realize in this very brief interchange between heaven and earth, that God was real, that He loved him, Loren, more than he could comprehend, and that it was time to give his life over to the Savior of the world, the Prince of Peace. Slowly he felt the stinging of the cold return, the biting on his face and hands. He grabbed for the park bench and struggled against all odds to stand up and brace himself against the back of the bench until strength could return to his limbs.

He wrapped his arms around himself seeking for warmth as he shuffled through the deep snow to his car that was all alone in the parking lot. He turned the key and heard the engine fire up. Not only was there life in the engine, but he also felt as if new life was being pumped into him.

Over the last several years as Loren's life was spiraling downward he had unconsciously moved closer and closer to the home he had known and loved. Many times he had wanted to reach out, to find that love again, to bound through the doors of his childhood home and say, "I'm home, I've returned!" But the prodigal son felt he had descended too low to be saved, too low to be welcomed home.

The park bench he had found himself sitting upon staring up at the stares of night was within a robin's flight of home. Through the tears that filled Loren's eyes, a mind still reeling from deaths hand, he found the street he had run down so many times as a child with his childhood friends and family.

Loren parked the car on the corner and braved the cold and deepening snow to walk the last hundred yards to his father's home. A large hedge surrounded the yard on both sides and Loren paused at the edge of the hedge his heart pounding in his chest. He could see the Christmas lights that were strung along the front of the house shining their mini lights into the night. He could see the multi-colored beautiful spruce Christmas tree in the window shining its light out as well.

And there, in the front yard, gazing upwards was the man who had loved him unconditionally. There was the man who had begged him not to go, who had taught him about character, and honor, and sacrifice. He was so still, so quiet, and looked so cold. Loren didn't know what to do. In his hesitation and agitation he rustled the branches of the hedge.

Andrew felt each little snow flake land on his face and then melt and run down his cheeks. He had been in the cold in the front yard for a very long time and was now aware that he was stiff and frozen. Just then he heard the rustling of some branches and looked towards the sound. He stared at it for the longest moment when a figure moved from behind the hedge towards him. The moisture and cold had made his eyes a little more difficult to focus.

As he watched this figure walk towards him he heard the words, "Dad," emanate from this figure. His eyes still unable to clearly focus, he recognized the voice. He had heard it many times in the past. The way it had formed the words dad, the way the inflection of the voice had pronounced that word, it was a little more deep, a little more mature sounding, but he knew it, it could be none other than his little Loren.

Without a moments hesitation he ran towards the figure and that voice and embrace Loren with all he had. He held on to him fearing this apparition would disappear as soon as he let go. He wanted to hold on to that figure forever not wanting to loose that moment. "Loren, Loren, my little lost Loren, is it you, is it really you," he heard himself cry out.

The choked words uttered the same response, "Oh dad, it is, is it really you whose holding me?" "I'm so lost and I'm so sorry for what I've been." They were the only words exchanged that frosty Christmas Eve night. Two men, one the father, one the son, embracing each other on a night where another Father had given His son to a world, to show that world, that he loved them so much that He was willing to give His only begotten Son in order to save them all.

With His arms still around Loren, Andrew guided him towards the house where warmth and love had been waiting for him all along. As the front door opened the warm air blew against the two frozen men and they knew that the warmth that they were experiencing was the warm air of the fireplace, and the warm aura of love that filled that heavenly home.

Loren was home again, he had returned. Just as the scriptural story of the prodigal son brought a fathers celebration for the return of that which was lost, so this Christmas day would bring the celebration of this prodigal that had returned.

And what is Christmas? Is it not the celebration of Jesus Christ, the Son of God, who was born in a lowly manger in Bethlehem? Is it not about His atonement and love that can and will reach down, further than we can ever fall, to pull us up and save us all? Is not this Christmas the joyous news that "For unto us a child is born, unto us a son is given: and the government shall be upon his shoulder: and his name shall be called Wonderful, Counselor, The mighty God, The everlasting Father, The Prince of Peace?"

I think that if every child could feel the love, and see into the heart of their parent(s) and know of the truths and wisdom that lay their they would not stray from the truths taught by those parents and they would cherish every moment with them knowing that all to soon the hand of death will separate them and the only hand able to reunite them is the hand of the Savior.

Return home young prodigal. Come home lost sheep. Have faith, feel hope, experience love, be converted, and live. Live a full life offered only through living a life devoted to God, to family, and to loving and serving your fellow man. Embrace the faith you have laid aside. Feel its power fill your heart again. Come feel the sweetness of the spirit and the overwhelming love of God again.

Merry Christmas.

The Sacrifice

Lisle sat cross-legged on a brightly decorated Christmas rug with their ornately decorated Christmas tree on the left side of her and a pile of shredded Christmas paper wrappings on the other. The heat from the crackling fire danced in the open-hearth fireplace and warmed the side of her face and shoulders. In her hand was an envelope. It was bound with a white ribbon and addressed to, "My Little Lisle."

After the seasonal songs about Christ had been sung, the Christmas story read, and the presents opened, there was always a letter to finish off the evenings Christmas celebration. At least that is how it had been for the previous eighteen years. This year would be no different, but it would be the last such letter she would get to open. This year, like past years, brought anticipation and excitement as she held the letter in her hands and wondered what it would say.

Gently she slid the white ribbon from the cream colored envelope and laid it on the rug next to her. Then, taking the letter opener from Sam's hand, she sliced open the fold of the envelope, and then she paused a moment to take a deep breath, as she did every year since she could remember, and pulled out the contents. Slowly she unfolded the cream colored paper and held it at an angle to the light of the fire so it would illuminate the page. "My dear little Lisle...," it always started out. As her eyes glided across the words on the page they would begin to fill with tears until they could no longer be held in check by her eyelids. Then, they would slowly trickle down her rose-colored cheeks and drip onto the page she held.

It had become a tradition; Sam would sit quietly in his well-worn wing-backed chair, and in silence, watch his daughter's face as she quietly read the words of the letter out loud. As her voice gave sound to the words a spiritual aura would fill the air surrounding both of them like warm thick air. Then that feeling would penetrate deep into the depths of their heart where it would seem to warm them up from the inside out. When she finished she would gently fold the paper back into its little square following the exact pattern it was originally folded in, and hold it in her lap and stare off into the flames of the fire. After a long moment Sam, her father, would bend over, kiss her on the forehead, and be holding two cups of hot chocolate and whisper, "Merry Christmas, and happy birthday Lisle."

The tradition began eighteen years ago on a wintery Christmas morning. It was a day of ultimate love. It was also a day of ultimate sacrifice, and a day of ultimate sorrow. Yet it was also a day of ultimate joy. How could so many conflicting emotions be rolled together in a singular event? Yet it was. However it had had its beginnings a year earlier with another joyous celebration other than that wintery Christmas morning.

Sam and Amanda had leaned across the sacred alter of marriage in the temple and kissed each other after they were pronounced man and wife by the sealer. They would always remember this day and have the honor of celebrating their anniversary and Christmas on the same day. It was the culmination of several years of fun, happiness, laughter, and then a long absence, while Sam was off serving a two-year mission for his church. True to her promise Amanda had waited for his return where they picked up where they had left off. Then there was more fun, happiness, and laughter. Sam wasn't sure his cup of joy could get any fuller. Every time he looked into his cup of joy it was full to the brim with happiness and satisfaction. He would seriously ponder how it was possible to be as blessed as he was. They seemed to match in every way, and in the rare instances where they did not; their differences complimented each other beautifully.

Love filled their lives. Amanda would randomly find a single red rose in a slim black vase in front of their bedroom door in the morning while Sam would find love notes with crayon drawings in his brown paper lunch bag taped onto his sandwich bag. Small kindnesses and courtesies filled their life. Even though money was a scarce commodity in their life, time together was not. Days were filled with thoughts of each other and evenings were filled with walks, board games, old movies, and just laughing.

Just when Sam and Amanda thought that their cup of joy could hold no more, their cup was enlarged and filled yet again with the announcement that a new baby would be on her way. The wonderful news filled both their hearts with excitement and gratitude.

Leaving the obstetrician they were elated when the due date was set on

Christmas Day! They realized that a baby can decide to come two weeks early or two weeks late, but they were really hoping she would decide to make it Christmas day. Then they could celebrate three great events on the same day, the birth of the Christ child, their anniversary, and the birth of their first child. "Just think," said Amanda, as they walked arm in arm toward the car, "if we could have all our children born on Christmas Day." "What a celebration that would be!" She laughed at the thought and laid her head on Sam's shoulder as he opened her side of the car door.

As the pregnancy increased so did their love for each other. They took a huge calendar and hung it on the wall in the family room where they marked off each day counting down toward the delivery date. As the months passed they made all the usual preparations for the new arrival, stockpiling diapers, onesies, bottles, and binkies. They searched out deals on cribs, pink sheets, tiny dresses, a car seat, and soft blankets. They each had a wonderful extended family that filled in the blanks.

The pregnancy had proved to be a challenge in endurance for Amanda. The first trimester was unbearable. Most mornings found her laying her face on the cool tile floor or leaning against the water closet heaving every other minute. The morning sickness pills took the edge off, sometimes. She was glad once she advanced into the second trimester when the nausea let up some.

Other than the difficulties with the pregnancy life could not have been better. Every morning before Sam left to work he would go through the same ritual. He would hold both of Amanda's hands in his, look her in the eye for a long moment, and exclaim how beautiful she looked, and how ardent his love was for her, and if she was going to be alright. He would then kiss her forehead, her nose, and then her lips. She mouthed the words, "I love you," and then he would walk out the door. She would wait right by the front door for ten seconds, and then it would open up again and Sam's head would pop in and asked, "Did I say I love you?" Amanda would simply lean over and kiss him on his forehead, his nose, and his lips.

As the pregnancy progressed into the late second trimester and early third trimester Amanda began to get more headaches and swelling of her hands and feet. The nausea returned and she struggled to feel better. The doctor diagnosed her with preeclampsia or toxemia. He prescribed more bed rest, magnesium injections, and a stricter diet. She endured this restriction on her freedom with patience and grace.

With the end of November the delivery date came into view. They had marked off December 1st on their calendar. Sam stood in front of the baby calendar with his arms around Amanda as they just stared at the X on December 1st. Very soon there would be a trio of happiness.

Their next visit to the obstetrician found themselves sitting in the doctor's office holding hands in adjacent seats listening to his concerns. He told them that Amanda had moved from preeclampsia to eclampsia and that her blood pressure was a serious concern and that her liver showed signs of serious distress and bleeding. He informed them that they were in a paradoxical situation with contradictory outcomes. "With eclampsia there is a very real possibility that either you, Amanda, or your baby, or both may not survive this pregnancy. Your health and your life is in serious jeopardy. The baby's health is in serious jeopardy as her lungs have not yet developed enough, and there are other fetal complications. That presents us with a decision that must be made."

Sam's countenance paled and his heart raced as the doctor spoke. He felt as if he were about to faint. His ears were ringing and his thoughts were clouding up. He fought to focus and think. Amanda squeezed Sam's hand and listened with calm attentiveness to all that the doctor was laying out. With a small quiver to her voice Amanda asked, "What is the decision that needs to be made?"

Doctor Matson looked into Amanda's eyes with such intensity that it seemed he would bore a hole right through her. She never flinched or removed eye contact with the doctor. His heart was filled with admiration and compassion for this young, strong wife, and mother to be. Clearing his throat several times, he finally said, "If we take the baby now, she will not make it. However if we take her now we will do all we can to save her, but you will have a better chance of surviving this delivery." "If we wait?"

90

asked Amanda. "The baby will have a better chance of surviving but percentages are still low that she can make it. However, your chances of heart failure, stroke, or exsanguination - bleeding out, go up significantly."

Every time Sam wanted to speak his voice choked up and no words seemed to be able to leave his lips. Amanda sensed his anxiety and could feel his agitated state. "When does a decision have to be made?" said Amanda, with a voice of strength that surprised even her. "Soon," responded Dr. Matson, "Absolutely no later than this weekend." "In a couple of days," repeated Sam softly, almost as if to himself.

Walking to their car in the chill afternoon December air Amanda again laid her head on Sam's shoulder as she did every time they left the doctor's office. Not a word was spoken. Amanda's heart was amazingly calm and at peace, while Sam's was whirling like a cyclone. Silence remained as Sam's hand gripped the steering wheel of their car so tightly his knuckles were turning white. His emotions were so entangled that he had no idea how to even begin to express what he was feeling.

The next several days were filled with conversation, prayer, worry, fear, prayer, conversation, ideas, and more prayer. No decision that either of them had ever had to make amounted to what faced them at this time. Even if a person lived a thousand years they are hardly ready to tackle such a decision. Yet that is what faced these two young people.

Laying in their bed between the warm covers, with the wind howling outside and the snow flying in flurries, Amanda rolled on her side and stared up into Sam's face. She could see his worry and anxiety. Softly she stroked his hair and in a tender voice, filled with assurance said, "Sam, I love you, you mean more to me than anything this world could ever offer. I love Lisle…" Sam looked down at her in astonishment at the name, as they had never come to any conclusions as to what her name should be and the name Lisle had never even come up!

He was about to comment when she touched his lips with her hand and continued, "Yes, her name is to be Lisle, it came to me in a dream last night. I saw her grown and beautiful and happy. She held my hand and kissed me on my cheek as tears flowed down hers. It's hard to explain, but we have a bond, one that transcends mortality or time. We are eternally linked together."

"Sam, we have prayed and asked for God's help in our lives and especially in this decision. I know what I am to do." Sam rolled on his side and put his hand on Amanda's cheek and responded with a sad melancholy to his voice, "are you sure you know it's the answer?" He knew his wife and he knew what decision she would make. He was afraid his nobility was not as great as hers. "Yes, I know what I am do to." She emphasized "know" with passion and fervency. "We will allow the pregnancy to go to full term and on Christmas day we will have the cesarean. We will put the event in God's hand and His will be done. If Lisle is strong enough she may survive, and if I am not too sick I may survive as well. I do not know God's ultimate plan or purpose for us, but this much I do know, that one of us will survive."

Sam's emotions already lay too close to the surface and his tears were wetting his pillow as Amanda spoke. He couldn't bear to loose her. She was his life, his world, his everything. How could he survive even one day with out her? He wanted to stand up and cry, "No, no, you must live!" But he could feel through her words, through her assurance, through the spiritual strength that filled the room that she was right. It was in God's hand. Everything is ultimately in God's hand, the world, the sunrise and sunsets, the sparrows in the trees and the lilies of the field. All are the workmanship of his hands. He created all of us and has a divine purpose for each and every one of us. This he knew.

"I am at peace," Amanda said calmly, "with whatever the eternal plan is for me. I want you to be at peace as well, however it turns out." She touched his face again and with her penetrating eyes said again, "Promise me, you too, will be Sam, promise me you will be at peace?" Sam squeezed his eyes together as if trying to prevent any more tears from falling out and in a half choked voice said simply, "Yes, I will."

Amanda spent her days on bed rest. With so much time on her hands, and not knowing what the ultimate outcome of their lives would be, she decided to write a series of letters to her unborn child. She wrote eighteen letters, which were to be opened every year on her birthday. Each letter would be a message of love from her mother as well as advise to her little Lisle during the different stages of her life. In her letters she would try and explain about her life, her experiences, her dreams, and how she felt about various topics. Hopefully the letters would not be needed and she would be able to be there to put her arms around her daughter and tell her these things in person.

As the twenty-fifth of December drew near she began to feel worse. Her headaches had reached an apex; she was nauseous and knew that she would not be able to wait any longer. As the night of the twenty-forth transitioned into the early morning of the twenty-fifth she awoke with an intense pain in the abdomen that double her over and caused her to cry out. Sam awoke startled with the outcry. "We need to go to the hospital," Amanda exclaimed in between moans of pain.

Everything had been prepared weeks before and Sam was able to keep his wits about him and successfully navigated them to the hospital in record time. In route Sam had called on his cell phone to notify the hospital of their situation and approximate arrival time. Upon arrival at the emergency doors a team of nurses met them and whisked Amanda away on a gurney to the emergency operating room that had been prepped.

The team of doctor and nurses began the emergency cesarean section with life support equipment for the infant as well as the mother. Sam was prevented from going inside the operating room and found himself standing in front of the stainless steel swinging doors just staring at them. His entire life was hanging on the fulcrum point of the great eternal plan. Would the pendulum swing toward Amanda, or would it swing toward Lisle, or would it swing away from both of them or toward both of them? The room began to whirl around and around and around until Sam found himself slumped up against the wall with his head in his hands.

How much time had elapsed? What had happened? Was the battle still being waged? Was it over? Was there an outcome? Bracing himself he slowly stood up and made his way to some seats that were next to a window that overlooked the lights of the city. It was still dark. Snow was falling and the large flakes were accumulating on the ground. Christmas lights which decorated houses could be seen by the hundreds as the people of their town were snug in their beds waiting the news that Santa had been there and it was time to open the presents and celebrate the magic of the day.

Sam wondered, as he stared out over the town, what would be his Christmas gift? Would he get the gift he wanted more than anything else in this world, his wife and newborn daughter safe? Would his cup of joy still be full to the brim, or would the cup be half empty, or emptied out? The anxiety ran high within Sam.

As he looked out into the lights of the city his mind reflected back again to the many nights, since the ill news was given them, he and Amanda had discussed the possible outcomes. The outcome was unknown, at least to them. To God, it was known, and was apart of His great plan for them. They did however know that there were four possible out comes; that they would both live, that they could both die, that Amanda could die, or that the baby could die.

In all four scenarios there was no choice. They really had no power to choose Amanda or the baby, or both or none. That choice would be made for them. The only choice they had was how to deal with the outcome. They could be bitter if it went ill, joyous if there was a miracle, or confused and lost if it played out differently.

The little choice that they did have was to decide whether to deliver early and add more risk to the baby, or to go to term giving the baby as much chance as possible but increasing Amanda's risk. In neither case was there a guarantee. They had discussed in detail the whys and wherefores of which life should be preserved if given the decision. They also discussed which of them should be given the better opportunity to successfully come through this ordeal.

In the end it was Amanda who crossed the bridge of decision. Her words echoed in his mind as they made the desperate dash to the hospital just hours earlier, "Sam," she gently said, "God has appointed a time to every person to die. We never know when that time will be, whether we will be old, or young, or a child, or even a newborn. We live our lives the best we can each day. We try to be good, to be kind, to help, to love, to feel hope, to dream. We have a vision in our own minds of how we think our life will play out. We see ourselves with children surrounding us laughing and giggling. Then we see ourselves with teenagers who struggle and we envision sitting up nights with them solving all of the problems of love and the unfairness of the world. Then we see grandchildren playing at our feet and us holding each other's hand, with gray hair, and the wrinkles of wisdom on our faces. And sometimes, those dreams actually happen, and sometimes they don't. But in the end it is ok, if we trust and have faith in that babe born in a manger in Bethlehem."

"I've thought of that babe, Sam," she continued, "many, many, times as I've lain in the solitude of our bed. I've thought about the baby Jesus and the good news that surrounded his birth and why we celebrate Christmas. But Sam, to me, it was much more. It ultimately was about this baby Jesus who grew up and who had a very similar decision to make. He was asked to sacrifice His life so we all can live. He overcame death and sin thus opening the door for us to live again, in joy, with God."

She touched Sam's arm and said, "Wasn't that a wonderful thing Sam?" "I am so amazed when I think of His love for me, and His willingness to sacrifice, or rather give, His life so I can live." He remembered how tears filled her eyes as she spoke of the feelings she had in her heart for the Savior of the world while enduring intense pain. Sam had pulled a hankie from his pocket and dabbed her eyes.

"I have been so blessed in my life Sam. I had a wonderful family growing up, I met the most perfect man in the world, and got to marry him, I've found the Christ that wise men looked for, and I have the privilege of bringing one of Gods daughters into the world. What more could I want?" Amanda looked Sam in the eye with such conviction and such love that Sam's eyes began to fill with tears. Amanda reached over and grabbed the hankie from Sam's hand and dabbed his eyes.

Sam turned and looked back at the lonely waiting room he was standing in. The white walls with pictures of happy moms and beautiful babies covered them. Ornate colored carpet, homey chairs, and bright lights filled the area. His mind once again went back to the ride to the hospital, "If it so happens Sam, that I am chosen to give the gift of life to our child, but it requires myself being sacrificed, I am willing to do so. I want her to have every opportunity possible to make it, and by us having held on as long as we did, I think we gave her as much of a chance to develop as we could possibly have. So I am very happy." As they pulled into the emergency entrance, Sam paused a moment and held Amanda's forehead to his and said, "I have prayed every morning and night that both you and Lisle will make it through this, and that we will have many years together to have gray hair and have the grandchildren play at our feet." Amanda half laughed and half cried as she embraced Sam with a firmness that said, "I don't want to leave you."

The decision had already been made, the course outlined, and now rested in the hands of a loving God, who knows all things from the beginning to the end, and has a wise purpose in all He does. This was their faith, this was their hope.

As Sam's mind came back to the reality of the here and now he saw the doors of the operating room open up and the Doctor walking towards him. Sam looked to the floor exploring the intricate patterns found there in the carpet. He did not want to look at the doctor's face and try to read what the expression was upon his countenance. He preferred to wait till he was in front of him and then wait for the words to spill forth.

Sam felt the touch of the doctor on his arm, and in a hesitant manner looked up into his eyes. There was sweat on the doctor's brow, and beads of perspiration dotted his forehead and his eyes had signs of red in the corners. He heard the strained, soft voice of the doctor, and struggled to focus on what he was saying. "Sam," a long pause came, and then his voice continued, "I am so, so, sorry. We did everything humanly possible to save your wife, but she simply bled out, and her heart stopped. We couldn't start it again. I'm, I'm, so sorry."

Shock, and silence were all that Sam could muster. He knew that this was a real possibility, but somehow, someway, he had hoped for a miracle, a different outcome, but this was it, this is what it was. He could feel the tears fill his eyes as he stared at the doctor. "What about Lisle, my little girl?" "How... what...," he couldn't finish the sentence, fearing he would be staring at a totally empty cup.

"She has made it so far. She is struggling for life, but is fighting with everything she has to hold on to it. It will be touch and go for a while." Sam found himself hugging the doctor and leaving tears of sorrow and joy on his green scrubs. The doctor simply put his arms around Sam and patted his back. Over his thirty years of medical service he had been in many waiting rooms dealing with the sorrow and grief of his patients.

Those early days and weeks of his new life without Amanda, but with Lisle, were filled with memories, sleepless nights, worry, fear, and hope. But as the years past and Lisle grew and the sharp pain of loss subsided he build a wonderful, joy filled life with Lisle. Each year on her birthday, his anniversary, Amanda's death, and Christmas day, they read a letter from Amanda to her little daughter, Lisle. As they read the words Sam could almost hear the soft, sweet voice of Amanda giving their daughter words of counsel, words of love, words of hope, and expressions of her feelings for her father Sam, and how much she loved him.

These letters were a treasure more valuable than any king's mountain of gold and jewels could ever be. In a way, Amanda had been there with the both of them through the last eighteen years. They could feel her presence when they laughed together, they could feel her unseen hand touch each of them when they sorrowed or struggled, they could sense her invisible footsteps as they quietly sat on the couch together and either read their scriptures, or napped, or watched an old movie. Yes, she had been with them, quietly watching over them.

They could especially feel her presence each Christmas day as Lisle opened the cream colored envelope and read the contents of the folded paper. Each time Lisle looked into the flickering flames of the fire she could see her mother's face smiling back at her. She knew Amanda was pleased with her, and her father. It was hard growing up without a mother, it was hard for Sam raising a daughter without a wife, but the sacrifice that

The Sacrifice

Amanda had made so little Lisle could live was worth every moment.

Lisle stood up from the floor, stared into the fire once more, and then turned and gave her father a huge hug and a kiss on the cheek, and put her forehead against his and stared into his tired eyes beneath a brow spotted with gray, and said, "I love you daddy! I will miss mom's letters. I never got to actually see her, but I have felt her many, many, times. I am so grateful to have had two wonderful parents."

He watched her as she went off to bed, grateful he didn't have to spend the last eighteen years alone. He leaned his back against the chair closing his eyes reflecting back again on a Christmas night eighteen years ago and a conversation in a desperate moment. The words of Amanda had come back to him, "If it so happens Sam, that I am chosen to give the gift of life to our child, but it requires myself being sacrificed, I am willing to do so." He reflected on her words, when the words of another man in a garden, kneeling in prayer, sweating great drops of blood from every pore rang in his mind as well, "O my Father, if it be possible, let this cup pass from me: nevertheless not as I will, but as thou wilt."

This was Christmas then, a time to love, a time to sacrifice for another, a time to give thanks for a loving God who knows all, and gave us the gift of His Son so that we all might look and live. To also give thanks for the sacrifices of other mortals in our life who were selfless in their actions as well. Life is an opportunity for all of us to learn the great lesson of life, "To love one another as I (God) have loved you."

Sam rose from his chair by the twinkling Christmas tree and made his way up to his room. He opened the drawer of his small desk and looked at the empty drawer where Amanda's letters had been for the last eighteen. His fingers touched the wood of the empty drawer. He held them there for a moment remembering Amanda's pen writing on sheets of paper trying desperately at times to think of all of the things a mother could possibly tell her daughter, enough things to last eighteen years.

Sam closed the drawer and walked over to the bed and pulled back the sheets and fluffed the pillows on Amanda's side of the bed, as he had done every night for eighteen years. He then pulled back the sheets on his side of the bed and fluffed his pillows. He then knelt in prayer on this Christmas night. As he knelt by his bed he could feel the presence of Amanda kneeling by his side. A warmth that was hard to explain unless you knew what the feeling was. He gave thanks to his Heavenly Father for the gift of His Son, for eighteen wonderful years with Lisle, and for a wonderful wife who gave her life so another might live. It truly was a wonderful Christmas.

The Sign

The chill of the December air seemed to penetrate through the fibers of the thin jacket, past the layers of fabric on the second hand shirt, and bite the skin. The harsh wind blew the wet and heavy snow sideways creating drifts alongside the parked cars and up against buildings. The wet snow didn't simply rest on the clothing of Michael but absorbed into his already wet fabric causing a shiver to emanate from him.

He put the sign down between his knees and folded his arms trying to warm himself by rubbing his crossed arms up and down hoping the friction would be enough to ease the stinging. Standing in place he wiggled his toes profusely inside his worn shoes. He then hopped up and down and stepped back and forth, first on one leg, and then the other trying to keep the blood moving.

As the traffic light changed he reached for the sign holding it up with one hand while shielding his ear from the biting cold of the wind with the other. His mind found it hard to concentrate, as all he could think about was how cold he was. A car filled with teenagers who had just left a near-by movie theatre swerved near the curb where Michael was standing and drove through a large puddle of water that had pooled next to the sidewalk causing the water to splash high into the air.

Michael was too busy trying to warm his ear that he did not notice the wall of dirty gutter water soaring towards him. The impact of the cold water splashing against his already cold and wet body sent him diving to the ground. As he lay on the snow-covered sidewalk he could hear the laughing of the teenagers as they sped away.

Brushing himself off as best he could, he picked up his sign, and tried to hold it with as much dignity as he could. And Michael Henson was dignified. He had seen men on street corners many times pan handling for spare change, scraggly men who smelled bad, and used the few coins generosity gave them to drown their misfortune in alcohol.

Yet every time Michael passed by one of these unfortunate wretches he had always pulled out whatever spare change he had and gave it to them. Sometimes it was a dollar and some change and other times it was a twenty. He never judged nor offered an indignant comment. He always felt a sorrow for these souls. He wondered more about what had brought them here than he did about whether or not they were going to waste his change.

Yet he was not here to get spare change. Although passers-by had given him $14.73 he was here to work. "I want to work," he would quietly reply, to the passers-by who offered him their spare change. "I do not want a hand out. I want to earn my money." His sign read '*Man with a family. Will work for food.*'

His father had taught him how to work, and to work hard. At ten years old he bailed hay on the farm right along with the other men. At fourteen, he got up at four o'clock in the morning to milk the cows, feed the animals, and muck out the stalls before he headed off to school where he carried a 3.8 grade average. After school he would hustle off to the local butchers shop to hose it down and get things cleaned for the next day's work.

He had worked hard and saved enough money to pay his way through college where he earned his degree. While in college he met the girl of his dreams Suzanne Baxter. She was a quiet, graceful person who radiated sunshine and had never spoken an unkind word toward anyone. And somehow she always managed to find something good in every person she met, including Trevor Chrisom. The only good thing Michael could offer to say about Trevor was, "the best thing I could say about Trevor is not to say anything."

Trevor was one of those people who always did it better, knew more, was sharp witted, and enjoyed contending with everything Michael did or said.

After several months of an idyllic courtship, Michael and Suzanne were married. A year later a baby boy was born. Then a girl followed by a set of twins, a boy and a girl. Another year past and another boy was born. It wasn't very long before the Michael and Suzanne Henson family was indeed a family with three boys and two girls.

102

Michael was able to land a job with a well known manufacturing company where he was able to put his education and talents to work. He was well liked by both his coworkers and his supervisors. After a short period of time he was promoted into a supervisory position in middle management.

It wasn't long before they were able to purchase a modest home with enough room for their modest size family to enjoy. Every evening as Michael passed through the doors of his castle he would look at his loving wife amidst their little army of toddlers surrounded by a disarray of toys, towels and toilet paper and think how lucky he was.

His life seemed to carry on in this blissful state for several years. He continued to save money, get promoted, and work hard. He was one of those rare individuals, who would, as the quaint saying goes, "Give you the shirt off his back."

When he wasn't playing Mr. Mom, helping with service projects at the church, or registering people to vote, you would find him serving someone. Sometimes it was Jim, the retired bus driver who broke his hip, and whose plumbing always seemed to leak. Other times it would be Billy, the little boy two doors down, whose muscular dystrophy couldn't deter him from letting his tricycle find the sticker weeds. And then there was Janis, the single mother of three children, and his neighbor across the street, who could not get her car started on a regular basis.

Somehow he never seemed to miss an opportunity to be of service. The perception in his neighborhood was that he must be a guardian angel in disguise as a Dad.

But as often as seems to be the case, when everything seems to be going well the proverbial rug gets pulled out from beneath the unsuspecting victim. And so it was with Michael. His wife had not been feeling well for several weeks. She was tired most of the time. A never-ending nausea was accompanied with an extreme lack of energy. Several times she would pass out for no apparent reason. Intense pains in her abdomen and numbness in her legs began to be a part of her daily routine. Finally Michael took Suzanne to the doctor.

After undergoing a battery of tests a tumor was discovered. The news, as such news always is, was received with astonishment and unbelief. Fear seemed to grip them both. Doctors offered their suggestions as to the treatment and advised they begin immediately. After prayerful consideration of their options they decided to go ahead with the advised surgery.

As they sat in their home with their children huddled up with them on the sofa, Michael and Suzanne informed the little family of their mother's health and that she would be going into surgery tomorrow. The risks they told their little ones, was great. But they were left with no choice. If their mother's life was to be saved, she needed the tumor removed. However, due to the tumor's position it was a high possibility that Suzanne might not make it through the surgery and at the very least, be left in a coma.

They decided as a family that since it was only two days before Christmas they would celebrate the birth of Christ that night the 23rd of December. A somber feeling permeated the room, but as if on a signal from a conductor, the Henson family, in orchestrated unity, surrounded Suzanne with hugs and kisses.

The celebration of Christmas that night filled the air. Songs of joy and hope engulfed the room. Laughter and giggling emanated from the children, good food graced the table and counters, presents were exchanged, and stockings filled. The spirit of Christmas filled their festivities. The evening passed almost as if it were a dream. The children filled their cups of Christmas joy to the brim. Never had their celebrations of Christmas meant so much. It was a lifetime of future Christmasses compressed into several hours. As the night descended the flickering of the fireplace found the Henson family asleep on the big feather bed in mom and dad's room seemingly unaware of the destiny that awaited them upon the rising of the sun.

Michael sat in the silent waiting room of the hospital, his thoughts were plagued by what-ifs. Every option was entertained by his thoughts, and they all caused him to shudder. He then reflected on his life, his precious time with Suzanne, and the fun filled days with his children. He then thought how good life truly had been. It was a life made happy with the wife he loved so dearly sprinkled with a collection of memories made sweet by his children. He had been blessed.

He leaned back and rested his head on the sill of the large paned window in the waiting room and closed his eyes. As his thoughts continued to race he realized he had no regrets. What a wonderful feeling. On the edge of a pivotal point in his life he was grateful for that peace.

Michael heard the approach of another person invade the stillness of the room. He looked up and saw the surgeon walking towards him pulling the gloves from his fingers. Michael tried to analyze his face. He looked for every nuance, a movement in his eyebrows, the slight shifting of his lips, or the furrowing of his forehead, anything to help him prepare for the words that were about to come.

In the stillness of the room the words "How is she," echoed out like a pebble hitting the ground in an empty cavern. The surgeon stopped and stared into the eyes of Michael. The pause felt like the eye of the hurricane, illusory and surreal.

Michael was told that the tumor was successfully removed but the surgery had left her in a coma. The surgeon continued that the prospects of her living through the night were highly improbable, and that he might want to spend a few moments with his wife before she passed on.

Michael stood in shocked silence, yes he knew this was a high possibility, and yes he had no regrets, yet the pain surged through his soul like molten lava. He slowly shook his head thanking the doctor for his efforts. With slow steps he made his way to the recovery room where Suzanne was lying motionless in the sterile room.

Michael slowly pushed open the door to the room watching as the light from the hallway slowly penetrated into the dark abyss. As the light rested upon the bed where Suzanne lay he could see the white sheet pulled up to her neck with a ventilator pumping oxygen into her lungs while the beeping of a machine monitored the beating of her heart.

The Sign

Michael stood at the doorway staring. His heart was filled with so many emotions he did not know which one to acquiesce to first. He stepped into the room allowing the door to close behind him. He did not search for the lights but used the small amount of light, which shone through the tiny window in the door, to illuminate his way to Suzanne's bedside.

He sat down on a chair next to her bed and held her hand as he laid his head upon her shoulder. Weeping, he slowly lifted his eyes to look into her cherished face. Her eyes were closed; yet peacefulness seemed to fill her face. He bent over and kissed her forehead while stroking her cheek. "I love you darling," he whispered, with a broken voice into her ear. "I had no regrets."

As the night passed he sat by her side reminiscing to her about all the good things that filled their lives. He told her about their first date on Christmas Eve, how they sledded down the snow covered hill crashing into a huge snow bank, getting the powdery snow down their backs, and how they rolled over each other with laughter. He reminisced about their greatest Christmas presents ever, the birth of their twins on Christmas day. He spoke about his love for each of their children and how he was going to miss her.

That night was the longest night he could ever remember. As the rays of the sun infiltrated room 4673, Suzanne lived still. Over the next several months she slowly began to take on some of the necessary life functions on her own. She had not awakened from the coma that held her captive but she was able to maintain life without the aid of machines and her brain waves increased to normal activity. Michael was finally able to take Suzanne home and care for her there.

As the time passed Michael tried to spend as much time as he could with Suzanne. He watched over her and cared for her. He attended to the duties of raising his children while maintaining a household along with his job. Although no matter how hard he worked things continued to go from bad to worse. His company had canceled the insurance, which was so vital to maintain Suzanne. The costs of her medical bills continued to mount

106

and eventually Michael felt as if he were drowning.

Even though his employer had a great amount of respect for Michael, they could no longer accept the continual absences and lateness and were forced to let him go. As medications and bills continued to mount, Michael could no longer afford the home he was living in and was forced to sell. His world began to close in on him. The strangling effect of the bills, the loss of work, and the inability to find employment in his specific occupation weighed heavy on his heart. He found it difficult to land a good paying job.

He took work wherever he could find it. One temporary employment agency sent him to a construction site where he was assigned to clean up the messes left by the workers. As he was making his way along scaffolding to dump a wheelbarrow full of debris, the board he was on snapped sending Michael plummeting to the ground.

The fall fractured his leg in several places. After weeks of recuperation he was finally able to get up and move around somewhat. The pain somehow never seemed to go away. As he tried to find work it became increasingly obvious no one wanted to hire him due to his physical condition and the circumstances he was in with a bed ridden wife who demanded constant attention.

Eventually Michael found a low paying job, which allowed him to earn enough money to pay for the minimal expenses of living. Yet there was so much more he needed. His children needed clothes and decent shoes, his wife required medication and medical supplies, food never seemed to last, and the heat was always kept extremely low. Unexpected expenses seemed to be the expected.

He finally decided to go to a busy street corner in his city and advertise himself for manual labor to see if he could acquire extra work until some unforeseen miracle might happen in his life to alleviate the tide of catastrophe.

He had seen through his eyes the forgotten souls panhandling for supposed work, he now saw through the eyes of a misbegotten soul who truly did want to work. In the eyes of humanity he had moved from the guardian angel disguised as a dad to the bum who should get a job.

He endured the sneers and ugly comments, the verbal abuse and disgusting looks. At night he worked his entry-level job close to home so if he was needed by one of his children or a situation with his wife arose he could be home at a moments notice. During the day he watched his children, ministered to his wife, and stood on the street corner with his sign lining up side work from compassionate people who were willing to help.

It was this day, the 24th of December, that he found himself on the corner of a street, the chill of the winter wind biting at his skin. In all the months he held his sign never had he given in to the utter feeling of hopelessness and despair that threatened to engulf him. Never in all that time did he utter an unkind word to those who passed by and reviled him. Never did he judge any man who did not offer his assistance. And never did he feel sorry for his plight nor blame the heavens or his wife for his misery. He never stopped loving his wife and his children.

No, his children did not know he stood on the street corner holding a sign, and of course his wife knew nothing of the incredible sacrifices he had made over the last three years. Nor would they if he had anything to say about it.

He was full of hope. In fact he believed that just around the corner was the train of hope. That just over the next rise was the green grass of relief. That tomorrow was a new day and that something good could happen. He believed that. He had to belief that.

Tomorrow was Christmas Day. He was hoping enough extra work would come from holding his sign, enough he hoped, to buy a special Christmas dinner for his beloved family. And if it were God's will he hoped for enough to buy each child a small gift.

However the blowing of the snow and freezing temperatures were enough to keep most people home. It became apparent he wasn't going to get much work today. The only people who seemed to be out in this kind of weather were the most ardent, which usually were those with nothing better to do like the car full of youth who were unkind.

Michael endured the conditions for the remainder of the day and a few hours into the evening. He desperately hoped for someone, anyone, to offer him some work. But as the darkness drew on, his ability to withstand the elements faded and he made the decision to return to his family. He knew his children needed him especially today. They had endured the poverty and trials well.

As he trudged through the wet snow he could feel a cold coming on. He was worn down. Too many hours of work, too many hours of providing all the needs of a destitute family, too many sleepless nights all began to take its toll.

He prayed he would be able to continue, as he was needed so desperately by a family that depended on him. His spirit began to weaken and his resolve began to wane. The spirit truly was willing, but the flesh was weakened. He looked ahead to the future and for the first time couldn't see the light at the end of the tunnel, and it scared him. So much depended on him, so much on his resolve and fortitude. But the weight became heavier than his emotions could bear and he felt the tears roll down his cheeks and freeze.

All the anguish, grief, and sorrow, created a melt down. The tide of tears could not be held back. Oh how he had hoped for a better time, a return to the avenue of joy. He wanted to return to a time when his efforts made a difference, a time when he did not have to see the sorrow in the eyes of his children, a time when he could hold Suzanne's hand and again feel her squeeze back, to feel her lips kiss back.

He stopped in his tracks and stared up into the heavens. He could see his breath coming out like smoke from a chimney rising into the air. He breathed in deep allowing the sharp crispness of the air to fill his lungs. He breathed in several breaths and held them slowly releasing the air held prisoner in his lungs.

He took another deep breath and looked straight ahead. The resolve poured back into his soul, determination filled his heart, and he walked home stepping more briskly through the snow-covered alley.

As he approached the building of his humble circumstances he saw a large black vehicle parked in front of his door the motor still running.

His heart started to pound as his imagination began to take over and fill his mind with visions of possible evils. He quickened his step almost running to reach his door. As he approached the car he looked inside but saw no one. He turned and opened the front door to his house. Stepping inside he froze.

There were his children sitting around a new table decorated with china, silver forks, and fine crystal stemware. An amazing Christmas meal was spread across the table. The aroma filled the air. Next to the table was a Christmas tree all decorated with strings of lights twinkling red and green. Ornaments of rocking horses, tin soldiers, gingerbread men, and ballerinas dangled from its branches. Presents glittering with red, blue, and purple foil wrapping were stacked around the bottom of the tree. And on the modest little end table was the most precious manger scene he had ever seen.

He could hardly believe his eyes. He looked at each one of his children as they sat at the table with smiles as big as the Cheshire cat. The excitement on their faces could hardly be contained. On the sofa next to the adorned tree lying as peaceful as she had over the last three years was Suzanne.

In his astonishment Michael noticed an older silver hair gentleman standing behind the table with a smile upon his face. Michael felt frightened, and then angry at the intrusion of this stranger into his home where his family was. Yet the man's warm smile had a familiar look, he recognized him from somewhere. His mind was racing trying to place a name or circumstance with the silver haired man.

Before Michael could connect who he was the silver haired man spoke. He explained that his name was Maximilion Carsdston, Max for short. He elucidated how he had passed Michael numerous times on the street as he held his sign looking for work. At first he didn't differentiate him from any of the other panhandlers begging for money. However after he had passed by him several times he overheard Michael's responses to people and realized he was an intelligent and polite person.

He continued, that it peaked his curiosity and he decided to follow him and see if he truly did perform the labors he advertised he did. He also followed him to see where he went. He explained he was sure Michael would go to the nearest tavern and spend the paltry change he had. But when he saw how hard he worked for people during the day and after a job was completed how he would go back to the street corner to hold his sign again until someone else needed some work. He decided there was something to this panhandler.

He found that Michael actually had an entry-level job where he worked the graveyard shift at a local warehouse, which was close to where he lived. He explained that his curiosity became even greater and that he decided to look into Michael Henson's life. He told him how he was amazed at what he had found. He said he was impressed with whom he had been and how he had contributed so much to the community where he lived. He told him that he had spoken to his neighbors and how each one had nothing but high praise for him and how they all had wondered where he had gone.

He explained how he had learned about his wife's surgery, Michael's accident, and the subsequent difficulties that plagued him. Max's voice then became quieter with a slight quiver to it which was accompanied by moisture filling up his eyes as he said, "I was so impressed by how you lived your life and how you faced your adversities that I knew I needed to help. I knew here was someone who truly deserved a miracle."

Max was one of the wealthiest men in the state. He had made his fortune in the oil industry. He had more money than he would be able to spend in several lifetimes. Never in that time had he heard a story such as Michael's. After explaining his story, Max asked Michael if it was all right that he had given his family the gifts he had. Michael stood in silence unable to answer as the tears filled his eyes.

Max continued that he had paid off all of his debts, and repurchased his home on the tree-lined avenue where he used to live but made a "few modifications" to the home. He also informed Michael that if he would like, he had a position for a man such as he in his company and that he would be well compensated for his time.

After he had spoken, Max, the silver haired gentleman, folded his arms, and stared at Michael with a warm smile. All Michael could do was cry. Not in his wildest dreams could he have ever imagined something like this happening to him. As he stood there tears flowing down his dirt-stained cheeks, his children flew off of their chairs and rushed to their dad surrounding him with hugs. They danced around him in a circle until they all fell to the ground and laughed and cried and laughed some more all the while Maximilion folded his arms and smiled.

Michael invited Max to stay and enjoy their Christmas Eve celebration. The singing of Christmas hymns permeated the room. The table was lavished with a plump turkey, pumpkin pie, hot apple cider with cinnamon sticks, and all the other dishes that taste of Christmas. They all gathered around the sofa where Suzanne lay and played games and laughed and sang and then played more games. The evening was filled with the joy of the yuletide spirit. But more importantly they all knelt down on their knees, the lights of the Christmas tree twinkling all around them, and offered a sincere prayer of gratitude. Never had the spirit of Christmas been felt more than that night in a rickety old house on a back alley of a run down part of town.

Michael, surrounded by his children, stood at the door of their rented shack and watched Max, the silver haired benefactor, drive off into the night. A new life was about to begin.

Michael tucked his boys into one bed and his girls into another and kissed each of their foreheads and wished them all the best of dreams on this special eve before Christmas. Turning off the lights to their room he stood in the doorway a moment longer than usual watching the light of the moon silhouette his children as they lay in their beds.

Michael walked to the couch where Suzanne was lying and sat next to her and held her hand. He stroked her face and told her all of the things that had happened. How a miracle had taken place and of his vision for a future life. No she did not understand him, yet he knew somehow that the sound of his voice comforted her in the dark empty room where her spirit was forced to stay.

Leaving the Christmas lights on he lay down beside her drifting off to sleep dreaming of dancing with Suzanne as they used to. This Christmas would be their last on the avenues of adversity.

Christmas day was one of thanksgiving and of just being together. They played games, popped popcorn, read stories, and ate a wonderful Christmas dinner. The children laughed, sang Christmas songs, read the story of the baby Jesus, and told stories of their favorite Christmas memories.

In the evening after all the children were in bed Michael sat next to Suzanne and just held her hand. He stared into her empty face and just thought. His thoughts were focused on the one Christmas present he wished he could be granted. He lay down on the sofa next to Suzanne holding onto her hand. As sleep began to settle over his mind he felt the slight pressure of a gentle squeeze on his hand from the soft hand of Suzanne. He looked up in time to see her eyes beginning to slightly open. Blinking several times she tried to shake off the cobwebs from a deep sleep. Her eyes searched the room trying to find something familiar to her surroundings. Finally her eyes landed upon Michael. Michael gazed back into her eyes in disbelief.

"Hello," she whispered, "Hello," answered Michael. "Did everything go well?" she asked. "Yes," Michael whispered back, "Everything went very well." He leaned over and kissed Suzanne gently on the lips moistening her face with his tears. He felt the tender touch of her lips as they pressed back against his. It was indeed a very merry Christmas.

The Search

The thin layer of frost on the inside of the old wood-framed window augmented the aura around the moon, which was shining in on a room full of sleeping children on the third floor of the state orphanage. Surrounding the muted light of the moon's image were tiny colored lights dancing around the glass from the reflections of taillights from the cars which passed by on the wet streets of Washington D.C.

The children were asleep in thin metal-framed beds covered with green wool blankets and small flat pillows with which to rest their weary heads upon. That is, all the children except one, Stephen.

Stephen's bed was the one situated below the frost-covered window. He lay wide-awake with his arms behind his head staring at the lit manifestation of the moon. As he gazed at the window he thought how much it looked like a big white Christmas light.

He imagined the wooden window was a Christmas tree, the dancing colored lights from the traffic were twinkling strings of bulbs carefully wrapped around the beautiful tree, and that the moon was an angel that graced the top of the imaginary tree.

It was Christmas Eve. He seemed to remember the smell of pine from a freshly cut Christmas tree. Cinnamon wafting through the air from freshly baked pies, and the scent of wax from candles, which were burning from a kitchen table. He remembered the sweet music that filled the air as carols were sung by a soft, gentle voice.

It was a dream from a far away time in a far away place. Each year these sensations were relived as if they were yesterday. He could not quite remember the players in the dream, nor where the heavenly place was, yet he could remember the feeling. It was like having a big feather comforter wrapped around him on a cold winter morning. Soft. Warm. Feelings he had forgotten.

He could not remember how long he had been in the state orphanage. It seemed like it may have been six or seven Christmasses ago. Many of the children he had known had come and gone. Some even came back again.

Nevertheless, he had never gone. Every year seemed to pass as the one before. Every Christmas Eve, he would celebrate the memories of Christmas' past below the frosted window.

One memory he had never forgotten was Danny, the little brother he used to have. He remembered holding on to him tightly when they first arrived at the orphanage. He did not understand exactly what was happening, but realized somehow that he was in charge of taking care of Danny. All he knew now was that he had failed. For days, he had walked around the orphanage looking for his little brother. He searched every room that was opened, looked under every bed, and checked every closet, but never found him.

Little Stephen had come to the orphanage when he was three years old. His little brother Danny was four months old. The orphanage was the only home he had known for the past six years. Stephen was never told his younger brother Danny had been adopted by a family only days after they had arrived at the orphanage.

Stephen knew he must have had a mother and a father though he was never told who they were, or what had happened to them. He was never told how they had left a Christmas party on a cold and snowy night six years ago on the twenty-fourth of December. How they were on their way home when they hit a patch of black ice causing them to lose control of their car. That the vehicle had spun in circles finally falling through the ice of an irrigation canal. That with the freezing temperature of the water and with the difficulty in getting out of the vehicle, they had both died.

Stephen and Danny were both waiting at home asleep on the couch with the babysitter in front of the freshly cut Christmas tree with all the multi-colored blinking lights illuminating the room. Freshly baked apple pies were still warm on the table awaiting the chilling news.

Stephen and Danny had no other surviving relatives. His grandparents had passed away many years before their parents' accident, and they had no aunts or uncles. No one was left to take care of these two little souls.

As Stephen lay on his bed in the dark, cold room the weight of his sadness pressed upon him. A tear rolled gently from his eye and settled in his ear. His little heart yearned for the joy and happiness, which were recessed deep in the corners of his memories.

Wherever this little brother of his had gone, he needed to find him. There was a yearning in his soul to find another living, breathing human being, who he could call family. He felt he was a part of something more. Not just a cipher that slept in the same kind of bed, wearing the same colored clothes, and eating the same meals as sixty other children, but a little boy that somebody really cared about.

He had never been taught about God, his love for his children, and how he sent his only begotten son to save mankind from sin and death. To save him, Stephen, a little, poor, ragged, love-starved, nine-year old boy, who lived in a forgotten orphanage, in a big city, with millions of people, and no one who really knew who he was and who would not care if they did. He had never been taught to kneel on his knees in respect, to bow his head in reverence, and fold his arms in devotion to utter words of sincere gratitude and desire to a divine being who was the Father of his spirit.

Yet there was some kind of an innate feeling, no, more than a feeling, an overwhelming desire to pray to an invisible deity that somehow he felt must really be in the heavens, someone who truly did look down on him, and did something no other person had ever done, care! Even though he had never been taught, at least in the orphanage, how to pray, he did indeed know how.

Every night this lonely child had knelt beside his metal-framed bed and uttered the words of a prayer that only a sad all alone child could utter. As he communed with God, he could feel the weight of his sadness lift a little. He felt that at least there was one person who did love him, and would give him hugs and kisses if he could. Prayer had given him the strength to face another day of emotional isolation.

It was those prayers that never let him forget the name of Danny. It was in those prayers that he would ask God if he would let him find his "little Danny." He had lost him and needed to find him, and would he, God, please show him where to look. Then he would climb in between the scratchy blankets and stare out his window into the stars of the night and hope for the day they would be reunited.

The bell in the room where Stephen and the other children slept rang loudly. As robots, they all climbed out of bed and shuffled in the cold of the morning to a breakfast of hot oatmeal and a piece of toast. It was Christmas day, a day just like any other. No Christmas tree, no presents with fancy paper and ribbons, no stockings with goodies, and no little manger scene on a table. The one thing special about Christmas in the orphanage was dinner. Not that dinner was different, but that they all got a little more than normal.

Along with a little more dinner was a little more free time. Stephen decided to spend this precious time in his secret spot in the big oak tree just past the grassy area next to the fence. Five branches up, the old oak was an area where three branches intersected each other and made a perfect spot for a person to snuggle up in. It was a quiet spot, one that made Stephen feel free.

From the vantage point of the high branch he could look out over the city. He would imagine himself as a large bird taking flight from the secluded haven of the oak tree and sail through the air, the cool breeze rushing past his ears, the air moving over his little body, his clothes flapping in the wind. He would see himself looking down on all the tiny people moving through the streets. He would sail over the monuments that graced the capital of his great country.

After his imaginary flight had concluded and he had landed safely in his bastion, he would then sit quietly against the majestic trunk of this enormous tree he called friend. Stephen laid his head against the bark and dreamed of finding Danny. Oh what a reunion it would be. He would run to him, scoop him up, and hug his neck. The tears would moisten their collars.

Then they would be taken into a beautiful home with a warm glowing fire and a Christmas tree all lit up, a huge turkey lying in the middle of a table would be surrounded by mashed potatoes and gravy, and all of the other fixings would join in to ornament the fine white tablecloth. Candles would be lit giving off a warm glow and make the Christmas dishes sparkle from the flickering of the candles. It was beautiful, not because of all the wonderful sights and smells, but because he was in a home, a home where love lived.

* * * * * *

Teresa Kensington sat by the fireplace in a large leather wing-backed chair, the light of the fire illuminating her face as she began opening the mail that had come earlier in the day. She was opening the many Christmas cards that came at this time of the year. As she worked her way through the stack of holiday greetings, she came across a white legal sized envelope with their address typed in an official font.

The addressee read Mr. & Mrs. Robert Kensington, 26 Maynard Court Washington D.C. She perused the envelope turning it over in her hands wondering who had sent it. There was no return address in the top left of the envelope. She grabbed her letter opener and with a mild curiosity sliced open the letter and pulled out the contents.

It was a multiple page letter. It began "Last known addressee:" As she read the words of the letter she could not believe what was written. "It couldn't be," she thought. "What a dreadful mistake." Her son, who was playing with a wooden truck next to the fireplace, noticed his mommy's sad countenance, stood up, leaned over the arm of the chair, and held her hand. "Are you okay mommy," he quietly asked, with a concerned look. Looking at his little face, she squeezed his hand, gave him a smile, and replied, "Yes dearest, we just received some sad news."

She stood up from the soft chair and looking at her little boy bent over and kissed him on the forehead and whispered to him, "I need to give daddy a call." She could not wait for Robert to come home from work. Immediately she went to the phone that was hanging on the kitchen wall next to the pantry. Picking up the receiver she cranked the dial several times. "Hello, operator, can you please connect me with Mr. Kensington at the Jefferson Towers, Washington D.C."

Robert's soft yet strong voice came across the phone. Teresa began to expound the contents of the letter to Robert. He could sense the anxiety in her voice. He knew she was deeply trouble by the letter as was he. There was only one thing they could do.

Robert spent the next several weeks making all the arrangements that were required to resolve this terrible oversight. He sat in his office staring out of the window at the lights of the nation's capital, which was all lit up with the decorations of the season. "What a tragedy," he thought. "How was it possible that something this important could be overlooked?" Everything was now in place to correct a mistake that had happened so many years ago. Was it too late? Would it make a difference? Would it all work out in the end, as his father use to say when he was a child? Tomorrow was the day when the three of them would have to put an end to this unfortunate circumstance.

Teresa checked the house over one more time to make sure everything was complete. Standing in the doorway, she looked back once more with tears in her eyes and closed the door. She turned the doorknob to make sure it was locked. This would be the end of their life as they knew it. Once she turned around a new life would begin. Would it be all right? Could she do what would be required of her? She walked to the car where Robert was waiting by the open door to help her in.

Before they climbed in, Robert held Teresa's hand and gazed into her eyes. He did not have to say a word. His eyes, the warmth of his smile, and the tenderness of his touch were enough to let her know it *would* be all right. Robert started the engine and backed out of the driveway. Snow began to fall. It *was* going to be a white Christmas.

* * * * * *

Stephen heard the bells of the orphanage ring alerting the children it was time for dinner. He had been sitting in his secret hideaway all afternoon. He watched as the snow began to slowly fall from the sky. The flakes were large and heavy and began to accumulate on the ground. The old oak tree looked like an island surrounded by a sea of white. Stephen climbed down from the tree and gradually made his way to the somber halls of the old orphanage.

The Search

With his head hung down, and his hands hidden in his pockets, he watched the footsteps he was creating as he walked in the freshly fallen snow. "One more Christmas past," he thought dejectedly. Another year and he still had not found his Danny. "Has God forgotten me," he sadly thought. "Has he forgotten Danny also?"

Reaching the steps of the old brick building he looked up at the steel doors, lights shining out through the tiny windows, and stopped. He stared at the entrance to the only place he could remember living, except in his dreams. He did not feel he could pass through the entry one more time, the passageway to despair, the passageway of lost hope, the passageway to yet another year of shattered dreams. He sat down on the steps and bowed his head into his knees.

Through the tiny window of the door Mrs. Hazleton watched little Stephen sitting on the steps his head hung in his knees. Her heart strained at the heartrending scene of this little boy who had been at this poor facility for most of his little life. She had seen many children come and go to families who were willing to take them in, families who were willing to add to their numbers, families who had love left over for another little soul. None of these families however, came for Stephen.

Mrs. Hazleton had worked at the orphanage since before Stephen had come. She was a good person, however she was busy and caught up in the duty of taking care of hundreds of children throughout the years. The great depression had created a great number of orphans. Parents who had passed away, parents who abandoned their babies, parents who could not afford to feed another mouth.

Sometimes the chores at the orphanage seemed so overwhelming it was a wonder they were able to provide the necessities that they did. Many a child slipped through the cracks. She had her own worries as well. Her husband had been out of work for several years and they struggled to put food on their table to support their four little children. There just didn't seem to be enough for one more.

She had a soft compassionate nature but was beset by the trials of life herself. However, as she stared at Stephen, her heart felt as if it were about to burst. If only she had the means. She would feel it a blessing to bring joy to this child. Of all the children who had been adopted, "This one," she thought, "this one would have been the dearest." It was almost as if he had been saved for someone or something special. She had wondered why all these years she had never noticed him. How was it possible for a human soul to simply be forgotten? To be alive, to move, to breathe, yet forgotten, to be unseen and unnoticed.

She did not force him to follow the schedule, to come in and eat. She turned and walked back into the recesses of the building leaving Stephen to sob on the step. She knew he just needed to be alone.

* * * * * *

The Kensingtons found themselves in a dark and gloomy building in a run down part of D.C. The building had been built at the turn of the century and had become somewhat dilapidated. The dingy white brick walls and dingy tile floors gave the building a septic, stale appearance. They presented the appropriate paper work to resolve the serious oversight which had been committed years before.

After several hours of negotiation and discussion, they were at last, able to get everything settled to the contentment of all involved. Teresa looked at Robert and gave him a large smile. He returned her smile with a nod of satisfaction. After the respectful farewells, the Kensingtons left the gloomy building.

As they drove back to their home on Maynard Court they were sad yet joyful. Everything had worked out well. They knew everything else would fall in place. Shortly, very shortly, another world awaited them. Teresa leaned her head on Robert's shoulder, as their little boy was asleep in the back seat unaware of what had taken place.

* * * * * *

Mrs. Hazleton returned to the lonely child she left sitting on the steps. Opening the door she descended the few steps to where Stephen was and sat down beside him. His head was still in his knees. For the first time she put her arms around his shoulders and stroked his hair. "Stephen," she whispered in his ear, "we need to collect your belongings dear. We have to move you to another location." He lifted his head and looked at her, "Ok, is it far?" "Not too far," she responded, grabbing a hold of his hand to help him up.

As they finished packing his meager belongings into a small trunk he stood at the foot of his metal framed bed and stared out the window. With a soft and low voice he asked, "Will you keep looking for my little brother? I have never been able to find him; I know mommy would have wanted me to keep him safe."

Mrs. Hazleton stood at the foot of the bed holding back the flood of emotions that was welling up inside of her. She had known the story of his little brother and had hoped he would eventually forget. He never did. She had. "Yes," she replied, "I will keep looking." She held out her hand for him to take. He put his hand in hers and they walked the gloomy, sterile, stale halls of the orphanage that was decorated with dingy white brick, and white tiled floors.

As the attendant drove Stephen to his new location he sat in the back seat of the car watching the streetlights go by. The car made turn after turn, went up a hill and back down, stopped at stoplights, and went on again. After what seemed like a very long time, the car finally came to a stop. The driver opened his door and walked to the trunk of the car. Opening the trunk lid he pulled out Stephen's belongings. A lifetime squeezed into one small trunk. After setting the trunk on the curb he came around the car and opened the door where Stephen was sitting.

Stephen climbed out of the big car, the chill of the air biting at his cheeks. Christmas Day was almost gone and with it, the hope he had held onto all these years, the hope of finding Danny. He was now being moved to another dark and gloomy place where he would be even lonelier. As he walked around the car to the curb where his trunk was sitting, he looked up.

He was not at a big dreary building, but a home with Christmas lights all around it. In a window, in front of this house, was a big pine tree twinkling with lights that wound all around it, and an angel was sitting on top illuminating the night.

He froze not daring to move. Was this real? What was happening? His eyes moved to the door of this amazing house. Standing in the doorway was a man, his arms around a woman, with a little boy about six years old wrapped in his mother's arms.

He looked up at the driver not knowing what was happening. The driver, a kindly old gentleman, looked down at Stephen and said, "this is your new home." Pointing to the family in the door he added, "and that is your new family." Stephen stood in the cold staring at the house and the people in the doorway not feeling the chill at all.

The Kensingtons ran from the doorway through the snow laden front yard and embraced Stephen. There he was in the middle of these people who were swinging him around and around. Kisses smothered his face, first from her, and then him, and then her again. The only thing Stephen could think to do was cry. And cry he did.

As Teresa and Robert held Stephen in the air between them they said to him, "We would like to introduce you to someone very special." The Kensingtons little boy walked out from behind his mother's coat. Stephen's eyes met those of the little boy. "This is your little lost brother Stephen, this is Danny."

The Kensingtons had adopted Danny six years earlier when his name came up as an infant who had just been placed on a list for parents who were waiting to adopt infants. No one had told them Danny had a brother. They were never given the opportunity to keep these two brothers together.

Holding his breath Stephen stared at Danny. A voice deep in his memory told him, yes, it is he, it is your Danny. Stephen ran to Danny and cupped his hands to Danny's cheeks and stared deep into his eyes with both their noses touching. He knew those eyes. He had looked at them many times when Danny was lying in the cradle. Stephen smiled, and then laughed as he scooped Danny up and hugged his neck. The two little lost brothers held onto each other tightly spinning around and around while the snow fell down from the stars on the two little boys. Stephen's laughter turned to tears. They were as the gates of a dam that had broken. Years of sorrow, sadness, and searching were being released. Danny did not recognize his older brother. However, a feeling that transcends this earth and its finiteness told him this was someone very important and special to him. The joy that filled the hearts of Robert and Teresa was indescribable.

As the emotional reunion in the front yard began to calm, the Kensington family walked up the yard, arm in arm, into the house. As they walked into the home Stephen could smell the scent of pine mixed with cinnamon. His senses began to be overwhelmed with the visual potpourri of Christmas. A fire was burning in the fireplace. How warm it made everything feel. And there, in the middle of the table, on top of a fine white tablecloth, lay a large turkey. Mash potatoes and gravy, stuffing, cranberry sauce, and all the rest, were spread out in-between the candles that flickered candescent light on the dishes of Christmas.

Truly, the great God, which lived in the Heavens, did answer little boys' prayers. Little boys whom everyone had forgotten, little boys lost in a sea of human despair. Indeed, this Christmas was a goodbye to a former life, and a hello to a new adventure called love. Love big enough to share with just one more.

* * * * * *

Mrs. Hazleton turned the lights out on the children in the orphanage silently wishing all the unfortunate souls a Merry Christmas. As she walked down the gloomy halls to go home for the night, she felt an immense joy she had not felt in years. She smiled as she opened the door into the cold of the winter night.

Walking across the frozen ground she did not even notice the chill of the winter night, her whole being felt warm. It was the beginning of a new life for her as well, a new way of looking at the unfortunate children of the world. She had found the joy in helping a child find his home. It was not easy. It took many hours of research and time. No one would ever know she was the one who had sent the unmarked letter to the Kensingtons letting them know a little boy was looking for his lost brother.

The Christmas Quilt

Nancy just finished pulling the last stitch through her Christmas quilt and tied the final knot. She sat in her old wooden rocking chair that she inherited from her mother, who inherited it from hers, whose husband built it. It was one of those chairs that sounds uncomfortable because it is made of wood, but this chair was special somehow because when Nancy sat in it she felt it was the most comfortable chair ever built. She had always commented on it and how she felt it was probably because three generations had sat in it and had worn it in such a fashion that it fit like a well broken in glove. Her grandmother, mother, and her were all about the same body size and build so the wear spots were perfect.

Sitting there with the quilt in her lap holding on to the corners of it with both her hands she held it close to her heart reflecting on the quilt which was more a project of love and identity than a cozy warm covering on cold nights, although it could definitely be used for that. She coughed a little and then leaned her head back on the old wooden rocker and slowly rocked it back and forth working through the pain.

Nancy had spent the last six months working tirelessly on this Christmas quilt. She wanted to be completed it before Christmas day and she accomplished this tremendous feat with two hours to spare. She turned her head slightly to the left so she could see the old grandfather clock next to the fireplace. Through the dim light she could barely make out the big and little hands on the old clock, it was 10 p.m.

It too like the old rocking chair had been handed down from the same grandparents to her and had been a part of her childhood memories. She loved the steady, calming tick tock of the old clock. It was a mesmerizing, soothing sound to her. To her it almost felt as if the old clock had magic in it.

Nancy rolled her head to the other side where a little end table sat next to her rocker. She reached for a bottle of medication with a glass of water that was sitting there. She held off as long as she could before she took its contents, as she wanted to be completely lucid in order to finish this quilt. The medication always made her very sleepy as well a nauseous most times. She decided to work through the pain in order to finish this oh so important gift.

She swallowed the two pills and laid her head back on the chair and stared at the Christmas tree, which sat decorated on the other side of the fireplace. She looked at each of the ornaments on the tree which represented memories and history. Each ornament was a handcrafted decoration made from either; wood, paper, wax, ceramic, or papier-mâché. Her great grandfather had unknowingly started this family tradition when he carved their first Christmas ornaments when they were first married. They didn't have money for the fancy department store decorations; so handmade was the next best option to nothing.

He had passed those handmade wooden ornaments to his son who liked them so much he added new carved ones to the collection. His children had then made ornaments out of paper in origami styles, and then others had made ceramic ones and then they were handed down and added to until it was Nancy's good fortune to have this entire priceless collection handed down to her as a tradition. She and her husband had also added to the collection with a series of papier-mâché ones depicting the manger scene with Mary and Joseph, the baby Jesus, the shepherds, sheep, wise men and even a star which now sat on top of the majestic fir Christmas tree.

All of Nancy's life was filled with tradition. Family was important, heritage was important, and traditions that help strengthen and helped remember family was important. This was why she wanted to make this Christmas quilt. Six months earlier Nancy was diagnosed with lymphatic cancer and was given only three to six months to live. It had already metastasized to stage 4 and there was little they could do. They began the usual treatments of radiation and chemotherapy all of which made her sick.

It was then that she came upon the idea of creating this Christmas quilt. She initially felt that there was hope in a recovery from this dreaded disease but as time went by she accepted the fact that most likely this was her time to go. It made her sad to think about it and most times brought her sensitive heart to tears. Not that she was going to die, she knew it was a part of life and that all human kind would have to pass through the door of death at some point to further their eternal destiny. No, her sadness wasn't for herself; it was for her little six-year-old daughter Mandy.

Nancy had gotten married a little later in life than most young women she knew. By twenty-two all her friends were either married with one child, simply married or were engaged to be married. Sometimes Nancy would lie in bed at night tears on the cusp of her eyelids waiting to spill over onto her pillow wondering why marriage bells had not tolled for her.

For whatever reason they did not toll for her till she was thirty. Through an unusual set of misadventures she had come to know Tad, a tall, shy man who had not had enough courage to ever ask a young woman out on a date let alone be married to one. But for whatever reason the two hit it off and became a match made in heaven. Somewhere deep down inside Tad had found the courage to propose to Nancy and from then on the tears stopped falling from her eyes and gladness began to fill her heart.

Not ten months later Nancy delivered a healthy little baby girl they named Mandy after Tads grandmother who had been a veritable influence for good in his life. He loved this little old woman, who was an immigrant from Romania, and who had always treated him with goodness and kindness.

Nancy continued to gently rock back and forth beginning to feel the effects of the heavy narcotic painkillers she needed to take. Her head began to swim as if in a sea with a storm approaching. She remembered well the day her beautiful little girl entered the world. The pain was great though nothing compared to now. As they laid the child on her chest all wrapped snugly in a swaddling blanket the pain she experienced faded from memory and she simply stared at the angelic face, the tiny little nose, the little dark eyelashes and the full head of thick hair. She stroked her precious little daughter's hair and kissed her forehead a dozen times each minute.

Her little daughter was the light and life of their world. They recorded everything, her first dirty diaper, her first cold, her first word, and her first steps. Nancy loved her little girl. Many times she couldn't wait for her to grow up so they could be best friends, but then she never wanted her to grow up and always wanted her to be whatever age she was at the time she had those thoughts as each phase of her life was a treasure to her.

They had tried many times to add more children into their lives but for some reason they were never able to have more children. Just months before her illness they had decided to go to an infertility expert to explore the possibilities of having more children. It was then that they thought there might be something askew and sent her for more testing. The results of that testing led her to visit an oncologist. The word alone brought fear into Nancy's heart. Tad was her strength and comfort and kept assuring her all would be well and there was nothing to fear.

But as life does sometimes, the dreaded word became a reality. A great sorrow filled her heart as they drove home from the doctor's visit. It was early May when the sun was high in the sky and the leaves were on the trees and the flowers were in full bloom as they drove home in a quiet, somber mood. Life had dealt them a hand they were not anticipating.

Over the next several months Nancy went through treatments and the series of emotions such news brings. She had relegated herself to the fact that she was most likely going to die. As she thought of that prospect her heart and thoughts went to her daughter, Mandy who would begin first grade this year. If the doctors were correct in their timeline she would not be around when Mandy started the second half of her school year.

Tears began to fill in her eyes as she reflected on that thought. Would her daughter remember her? Would she remember the times they had laughed together, played together, and read books together? Would her heart remember how it felt when they ran in the grass together playing red light green light and Mother-May-I? Would she remember the kisses on her cheek then forehead and then cheek in that order as she kissed her goodnight? Would she remember how they cuddled together on the couch next to the fireplace after her baths while she was still wrapped in a large soft white towel, probably not? This would then make her tears flow even harder.

It was then that she knew she had to create a keepsake that she could pass on specifically to her little girl that would help her remember who she was, what they did, and what she wanted to tell her in her future years to help her through the stages of her young life. Rocking in her favorite wooden rocker one painful night when she couldn't sleep she came upon the idea to create a quilt.

Her doctors had told her she probably had four to six months left. She knew sometimes the doctor's timetables were off. Sometimes the patient dies sooner, but sometimes they lived longer. That became the hope she would cling to. She would use that hope to create a Christmas quilt and with God's blessing, finish it by Christmas day, in order to give it to her daughter so she could tell her about the knowledge and memories that were a part of the quilt.

In between good days and bad days Nancy sketched out what would make up the quilt. Each patch would contain something different. The first row would be special memories to help Mandy remember who her mother was. There was a patch with green threads of yarn next to a house with the two of them holding hands in the grass. There was patch with embroidered books on it with titles such as Peter Rabbit, Charlotte's Web, and the Wizard of Oz. Another patch had a Christmas tree and a doll sitting under the tree another patch had a stove, some eggs, and a pot sitting on it. And there would be a patch of snow falling with a sled racing down a hill.

The next row would be patches to help her through the first year of her mother being gone. There would be a patch with a picture of Jesus on it. Another patch would have a picture of Tad with Mandy sitting on his lap reading a book. There would be a patch of a puppy dog's front paws down wrestling with a bone. A patch with angels flying over a little child in a bed, a patch of Nancy kneeling next to a bed with Mandy next to her praying to a loving Heavenly Father who knows her name.

The next row would help her through her childhood years as a young girl. She sketched a patch with pretty pink shoes with lovely bows on them, a patch of a church with lights coming out from the doors, a patch with a toothbrush and toothpaste on it, a patch of a little girl by herself praying next to her bed, and a patch of the same little girl holding a little doll sitting next to a fireplace with glowing flames.

She would have rows to help her through her adolescent years, late teens, dating and on to getting married. She would have a patch of having children, of living faithfully to your convictions, of motherhood and its joys and challenges. There would be a patch with a sink full of dirty dishes, of flower beds outside of a house, of laundry neatly stacked next to the washer and a pile of dirty clothes on the floor in front of it, of a mother chasing after a little one with a diaper, and of a mother in a rocking chair holding her sleeping child.

This quilt would be a lifetime compressed into fabric. A lifetime of past memories lived, a present with the wisdom garnered in a young life faced with monumental challenges, and of a future that would never be but anticipated as to what it could be. It was a wife's wishes and a mother's dreams for her daughter. It was a patchwork of illustrations formulated to tell a story of a mother's love for her daughter. It was a collection of visual parables that would allow herself to be a part of Mandy's life long after her physical body had been laid in the ground and covered with mother earth.

Nancy wanted Mandy to know through this quilt that she would always be there in spirit with her. She would be watching over her, encouraging her, whispering spirit-to-spirit words of comfort and healing when difficult times would arise in Mandy's life. Every time Mandy would cuddle up with the quilt she wanted her to not only know that her mother loved her, but that she still loved her. She wanted her to feel that love radiate through her via the warmth of the quilt.

As her head rested on the old wooden chair she felt the tiredness permeate through her entire body. The drug was finding its way into her bloodstream and began to course throughout her body masking the effects of the pain, a disease that centered in the cells of her body turning into her enemy, slowly and relentlessly strangling the good cells of their life and shutting down the entire bodily system. It was an odd feeling to know that you were slowly killing you.

Her eyes began to slowly close. The lids of her eyes felt as if each one weighed fifty pounds. It was a monumental task to try and keep them open, but Nancy wanted to keep them open just a little bit longer. She wanted to visually take in the sights of Christmas before she slept. With every ounce of strength she fought to look at the wonderful Christmas tree, and to try and count each ornament that dangled there. She moved her eyes to stare at the manger scene below the tree and identify each character in the scene. How many sheep were there, how many shepherds tended the sheep, where were the wise men standing, was that a camel behind the manger, and was Mary on the left or the right of the baby Jesus lying in the wooden manger? Where was the star that shone bright that night?

Her eyelids closed for a moment and then with great effort again she opened them and rolled her head to the other side and looked at the colorful wooden nutcracker sitting on the end table, which her husband had brought back from Germany, where he had served a mission for his church. The stately nutcracker sat next to the angel carousel that spun in mesmerizing circles when the candles below them were lit. She watched the tinkling angels rotate and followed the reflective lights as they spun in a circle. Lastly her eyes fell on the old bible that sat on the same end table with the page open to the book of Luke wherein was the story of the birth of the Savior of the world.

Her eyes were now too heavy to keep open. The effort was now past her ability to fight and she slowly relaxed and accepted the inevitable. Yet her mind however was not yet asleep. It reflected back to the second chapter in the book on the end table and of a priceless gift that a loving God, a Father in Heaven, had given to all his children. The gift of a perfect son, part God, part man, to help each one return back home to Him. A gift that could heal, comfort, bring peace in turmoil, and lighten burdens. It was this gift that meant so much to her in her final months of mortality. It was this gift that she hoped would be passed on to her daughter. Even though she had suffered and felt fear and sorrow at times, her overarching feeling was that all of life had meaning, purpose and value. She knew where she had come from, she knew why she had been on earth, and she knew where she was going once the final count of terminal cells had conquered the good cells.

As her mind began to shut down her last thoughts were of a beautiful six year old who earlier had run up to her mother holding her face in her tiny little hands and kissed her goodnight telling her how much she loved her mother. "See you in the morning mama," she had said, as she scurried away to bed. Little did that small bundle of joy and love know that the quilt that lay in her mother's lap would be her last memory of seeing her mother alive.

Nancy passed sometime during that night. Her transition from mortality to immortality was peaceful. Her life had not been a long one, but it had been a full one, one of learning, of usefulness, and of love, it had been a life with deep meaning. Her prayers to God had been answered and she was able to finish her Christmas quilt. Wrapped up, beneath the tree, in silver and blue paper with a red ribbon on it, was a handwritten book. Within it's pages were a description of each patch as Nancy had envisioned it when she designed the Christmas quilt. It would be a precious keepsake for an energetic, bright eyed six year old who would have her mother with her throughout her life to teach her lessons, give her hope, and invite comfort on cold nights.

It is true that when a loved one passes away we shed tears of sorrow for the times we will not have. We miss them and have an empty feeling in our soul for that person. We look forward to the time, possibly in the far distant future, where we will reunite in each others arms and the passing of time will seem but a small moment. Mandy cried big tears for days until her eyes had no more tears and her head hurt. But days turned into weeks which turned into months and then into years. The sadness left and was slowly replaced by life and living and the future and of dreams being fulfilled.

Marriage came, children came, and nights in a well worn rocking chair with a sleeping child in arms came as well and through it all a patchwork Christmas quilt showed signs of wear and fraying around the edges. For Mandy it had been a large part of her life. It had been hope, it had been comfort, it had been answers, and it had covered little hands and little feet on cold Christmas evenings. One can only assume that a loving mother looked down from above on another loving mother's life and was so grateful she had time to finish a quilt for Christmas.

Yes Nancy had been there through it all. She had been apart of Mandy's life; a part of her husband, Ben's life, a part of six grandchildren's lives, and was now apart of great grandchildren's lives. Soon Mandy the energetic little six year old would return home as well to the embrace of a mother who thought enough of her to leave apart of her with her. And so the Christmas quilt touched many generations, as did the old wooden rocking chair. It was rare to see the two without each other especially at Christmas time blessing yet another generation of lovely little lives sitting in the rocker wrapped in a quilt looking at the lights of Christmas and a colorful nutcracker with an old bible opened to Luke chapter two.

A Life Lived

Bursts of smoke accompanied with loud explosions lit up the night sky illuminating the cockpit of the B-17 Flying Fortress. Eldon looked at his chronograph whispering to the instrument panel that they only had two more minutes to the drop zone.

The Japanese were sailing their fleet to Bataan in the Philippines preparing for an invasion. Eldon along with the nine other members of his crew were dispatched from Manila, along with several other bombers and fighter escorts to attack the Japanese fleet while en route to Bataan.

His thoughts, at that moment, were focused on a small farm house in western Nebraska where, among the falling snow and the starlit night, his mother and father would soon be gathering the family together to sing the traditional Christmas songs and read the story of the Christ child from the Book of Luke.

Gathering around the candle lit tree would be Sara his older sister along with Steven and James his two younger brothers. They would be celebrating the joys of the Christmas season. Presents would be exchanged, laughter would fill the air, and the most famous home cooked meal in all the world would be served to the attending members of his extended family who would travel from across the plains of wheat and corn to share in the celebration.

Christmas time was one of Eldon's favorite times of the year. He could never really put his finger on exactly why it was his favorite time; it was probably a montage of many things. He loved the color of the snow when the red, blue, green, and yellow lights blinked from atop the house. It gave the snow an almost dazzling brilliance. He loved the Christmas tree, which was decorated with homemade ornaments from years past and now became a history of Christmas past. He loved the red and white candles, which would be burning throughout the house illuminating each room in a warm glow of golden light. He loved the carolers who would come around each twenty-fourth of December and stand below the street lamp just as the sidewalk met the porch of their home and sing "O Holy Night." He loved the turkey, the stockings hung by the chimney with care,

the chocolate Santa's, sleigh rides in the town square and the beautiful wreathes on the doors of each home in his little town.

But most of all, he loved Christmas because he loved family, he loved his neighbors, he loved the Christ child in the manger, and he loved how the season seemed to bring out the best in everyone. For some reason people seemed a little nicer, they were more friendly, they seemed to show more courtesies and have more patience with others short comings. It truly was the most wonderful time of the year, just as the song described.

Another burst of light along with an explosion shook the plane as it roared towards the oncoming fleet. Eldon looked again at his chronograph and picked up the microphone and held it to his lips for a few seconds as he finished the last remaining visions of his Christmas reminiscence.

This December found him in the middle of world war two where once again a world had to come together to throw off some more tyrants. It seemed to him that the world was getting weary of dictators, and despots. Every time an oppressor would rise up hundreds, thousands, and even millions of people died. If only every one could understand Christmas and its supernal message he thought.

He pressed the microphone to his lips and over the roar of the engines and the noise of the bombs bursting around the flying fortress Eldon ordered the crew to prepare for the upcoming target. The bombardier, ball turret gunner, waist gunner, and tail gunner replied back that they were in position with guns loaded.

The ten men who were the able crew of this flying fortress so aptly named the Merry Belle were all men that Eldon had flown with since their training at flight school. They had flown over fifty missions together and were well weathered in the art of aerial battle. Eldon felt a keen sense of camaraderie with these men who had survived many direct hits and through what he called, "the grace of God" returned home to base when no other logical explanation could explain how their B-17 was able to stay in the air.

As they approached the fleet, the flight engineer spotted a dozen Japanese Zero's closing in on their squadron. Within seconds machine guns could be heard strafing across the skies. The P-51 escorts winged out of formation and began to engage the incoming Zero's.

Bombs, bullets, and smoke filled the air as the racing of the engines sped the bombers over their targets, The bombardiers opened the bottom hatch of the plane and carefully sighting in the Japanese ships let loose their payload of bombs from the belly of the plane. Flames lit up the night as their targets were hit one after another.

Among the noise, clamor and adrenaline the Merry Belle was strafed with a line of bullets, which tore apart the metal fuselage ripping into the interior of the plane. Screams could be heard as several of the crewmembers had been hit and killed instantly. Within several more minutes a second and third enemy fighter plane had opened their barrage of bullets upon the Merry Belle and soon two of the four engines were in flames.

Their payload had been dropped and Eldon banked the B-17 sharply to the south and was desperately trying to head back to the island of Luzan where he would try and find a suitable landing spot for the flying fortress which was no small feat. As they were attempting their escape their plane was pelted one more time with enemy bullets. Smoke was now billowing profusely from the fuselage of the plane and was filling the lungs and eyes of the crew with thick black smoke, which was overwhelming.

Through the smoke and flames Eldon managed to find a spot within the jungle that with a miracle he could land the Merry Belle. As the monstrous plane roared above the tree line of the island Eldon pushed the stick forward and the flying fortress dropped into the jungle and crashed onto the jungle floor sending the B-17 skidding along the foliage sideways for hundreds of yards before crashing into a thicket of trees abruptly stopping the plane.

Eldon held the miniature replica of the B-17 flying fortress in his hands as he remembered every detail of that disastrous landing sixty-seven years ago. He had taken that small model of the plane he once flew and had put a string around the tiny fuselage and hung it on his tiny little tree, which sat, atop his small little kitchen table.

As he hung the ornament on the bare tree a tear rolled from his moist eyes and down his wrinkled cheeks following the groove time had worn into his rugged yet gentle face. He slowly bowed his head and silently said a prayer for each of the crew who had lost their lives in that fateful battle in December 1941. He had done this every Christmas ever since. He did not want to forget those young men who like himself had a whole life of adventure and dreams ahead of them. Instead these young men had died in a piece of flying metal, or in a hot humid jungle mud caked in their hair and on their sun burnt skinned.

He gently touched the outline of the plane one more time before he reached into the small cardboard box, which sat on the rickety wooden chair next to the table. The tiny box held a small quantity of ornaments, which Eldon had saved over the years. Ornaments that had meaning and memories associated with each one. As the years passed and the world he knew slowly changed the superfluous ornaments somehow had either gotten broken, disappeared in the passage of time, or had simply been given to goodwill to ease the burden of continual storage.

As he reached his old tired hands into the box he grabbed another ornament and pulled it into the less than bright light and looked at it. It was a simple piece of wood only three inches long with 731 notches carved into the stick. It was worn and smooth, as it had been polished with oil from the hands of Eldon as he held and rubbed the tiny piece of wood for comfort each of the 731 days that he carried it in captivity.

It was a reminder of a nightmare he had hoped to wake up from yet every morning his vision was filled with the same dirt and dying men. Eldon held the smooth stick between his fingers and rubbed it gently as he had done hundreds of times during the Bataan Death March and his subsequent imprisonment at Camp O'Donnell. He held the wooden memento up to his nose where he could still smell the jungle air and rot of the prison camp.

The smell enlivened his senses to the point that he could hear the sounds of the rain falling and beating upon the grass huts and the moaning of the sick soldiers suffering with dysentery, and the harsh commands

of the prison guards shouting their orders at the weak men. The feelings so overwhelmed him that he fell softly into the companion chair next to the one with the ornament box resting on it.

Eldon closed his eyes and recalled his first Christmas as a prisoner of war. He knew it was Christmas because he had notched each day into a tiny piece of wood he had found on the jungle floor. After they had marched fifty miles in the heat over broken roads with little water and no food he had fallen to the earth with heat prostration feeling as if he were about to die. His eyes had reopened after he was hit several times with a bamboo stick and the first thing his eyes landed upon was this little piece of wood.

He never thought he would survive the ninety-mile march but he did. Many thousands had died along the trail. Eldon had wished many times during the years of his incarceration that he could have died. But that little stick somehow gave him hope.

This first Christmas at Camp O'Donnell was not the Christmases he had remembered what now seemed another lifetime ago. Yet he remembered what Christmas was about. He remembered a tiny babe born in Bethlehem in a manger because there was no room for them in the inn. He remembered what this tiny child had done once he had become a man. How he had healed the sick, raised the dead, forgave the sinner, and loved the poor. He remembered that the Christ had died for him, and in all this remembering he felt hope.

Hope that came to him in a place filled with flies, rotten food, contaminated water, rags for clothing, and a reed mat for a bed. Yet there was hope in a place of despair. This Christmas he had imagined his tiny stick as a mighty fir, and his notches to count the days as decoration on the mighty fir, it was his very own Christmas tree. He stuck the little stick in the dirt next to his mat and had taken a couple of grains of rice and placed it beneath the stick for a representation of gifts. He imagined his family gathered around him filling the air with music.

It was this Christmas that he held Lance, the turret gunner, in his lap trying to comfort him, as he was delirious with the final thralls of malaria

and starvation. Every member of the Merry Belle had either died when their plane was riddled with bullet holes, or along the Bataan death march, or in the prison camp. Eldon gently rubbed his fingers through Lances hair and wiped the sweat from off his forehead, as he lay curled up in his lap. He was dying and it wouldn't be much longer before he was released from this earthly anguish.

Eldon reached down and held the mud-stained fingers of Lance. He pressed them firmly with his, yet with gentleness, conveying to him that there was still another human being in this hellhole who still loved him and who would still show him kindness. After all, wasn't this really what Christmas was all about?

Eldon stood up from the chair and placed the ornament on the tiny tree and then stood back a pace or two and just looked at them. After a moment or so, he went over to the kitchen sink and turned on the hot water and let it run until the water was steaming. He opened a packet of hot chocolate and poured it into a mug and then filled it with the steamy liquid.

He blew into the cup several times and then raised it to his lips and sipped the hot drink. He then reached into the little cardboard box again and pulled out a wedding ring. A string had been tied around it so it too could be hung on the Christmas tree. It was a simple gold band with a very small diamond on a mount. It wasn't elaborate, or fancy, or for that matter even expensive, but it had graced the finger of the most wonderful woman in all the world.

He placed the ring in the palm of his hand and stared at it against the age spots, which dotted his hands. This simple ring had sat upon the finger of Marian, a kind hearted and gentle woman who Eldon had met at their church's Christmas party several months before he was drafted into the Air Force. It was one of those truly rare moments in life where love at first sight actually happened. They were both enamored with each other. Neither was what the world would term handsome or pretty, but both Eldon and Marian were the type of people that every one would want to know and if fortunate enough would be a friend with.

People couldn't explain it, but there was just something about them that made you feel important in their presence. They were always kind, and when they spoke there was a calmness and an assurance which permeated the air around them.

Eldon had fought through the thirst, the starvation, the disease and despair, so that he would one day be able to see her again.

Marian had received a telegram that December day that Eldon's plane was shot down that he was missing in action and was presumed dead. Marian had kept hope going in her heart for close to three years, feeling somehow, against all of her family and friends advise to move on with her life, that Eldon was alive. She couldn't explain it, but she just knew he was.

As Eldon held the ring in his palm he remembered well when the opportunity presented itself to escape when they were being transferred from Camp O'Donnell to Cabanatuan. All of the soldiers were being relocated to this camp. Some how in the transfer there was a singular moment in which there was chaos and attentions were diverted and Eldon took that instant to fall down and roll into the thick jungle brush and hide himself beneath a rotting log for hours in the moist mud. He made his way south to Manila, where he hid and lived off of bugs and jungle fruit till General Mcarthur landed back on the Phillipines in October of 1944.

Eventually the war had ended, and Eldon was able to marry Marian, the love of his life. It was a modest ceremony, both kneeling at an alter across from one another, holding hands and smiling at each other with tenderness. Vows of eternal love and commitment were exchanged and a simple gold ring with a tiny, tiny diamond was placed on the petite finger of Marian. Marian held her hand in the air and looked at the ring as a smile graced her smooth face. To her it was the most beautiful object ever created. As the years of her life advanced she would still periodically hold her hand in front of her now lined face and smile still thinking it was the most wonderful thing she possessed.

A new life had begun. The years were filled with simple joy. Somehow children never blessed their home even though many tears of anguish were shed over the years of hoping and waiting. Their years had not been wasted with sorrow and blame but were abundant and rewarding. They had filled their days with serving mankind. They volunteered their time in foster care, in scouting, at their church, and in many community service projects. Some said that the angels above were nervous they would loose their jobs.

Eldon took the precious ring from his hand and tenderly kissed the ring and then hung it at the top branch of his little Charlie Brown tree. Tears filled his dim eyes as he looked at the ring. Through the tears the ring seemed more brilliant than ever.

Eldon knew sorrow, he knew hurt, and he knew sadness. His life had been filled with experiences so vast and varied that volumes could be written about such a life. Yet as the years past, friends and loved ones had passed away as well. Those he knew and who knew him were gone. A once rich and acknowledged life had now past into obscurity. He lived in a small and very modest apartment in an unassuming part of town. His entire life was now packed into a two-room single bath accommodation. Forgotten, alone, and unknown Eldon stood in the kitchen of his hovel hanging memorials from a tree that looked more like a starved branch of a scrubby tree.

As he stood and wondered at the brilliance of the ring he had hung from the tree his mind was transported to a spacious sun filled room at the top of a flight of stairs in a place he had called home. Lying on a feather filled bed covered in a white cotton comforter was Marian. Her face was pallid, her frame was thin, and her hand trembled as Eldon held it tightly in his own. She had always wanted to pass away on a beautifully sunny day in the spring, and it looked as if her wish would be granted.

Eldon's eyes were once again filled with tears. It seems as if he had been at the side of many a person who was leaving this mortal existence. Each time it felt as if the person were going home and he was being left behind. Only this time the feeling of aloneness was so over whelming he felt as if a dark cloud was swallowing him whole. Marian's eyes had briefly opened and she saw Eldon's white haired head hanging down with drops of water falling upon the white cotton comforter. Her heart ached for him.

She knew how much sorrow his life had seen. She also knew how important she was to him, and that loosing her would break his heart into pieces.

She pulled her frail trembling hand from his and stroked his hair. She
ran her fingers on his cheeks and across his lips. Eldon held her hand and
kissed it time and time again. Her mind struggled to find the words to
comfort his heart. After a time she feebly whispered for him to remember
the first Christmas they spent together after they were married.

He raised his eyes to meet hers and let his mind roll along back in
time to that Christmas night. They were young, happy, and excited to be
alive. They both stood facing the Christmas tree hand in hand the lights
of the tree illuminating their faces and reflecting off of their eyes. They
decided at that moment the lights of the Christmas tree for them would
represent their eternal and burning love for each other, a light that would
never go out, a light that would always burn bright.

Eldon could hear the soft words of the vision echo in his ears that as
those lights burn brightly illuminating the tree so would her love for him
always burn as bright and help to illuminate his life. She whispered that
death was not the end but another beginning for them both and even
though they would be separated for a short time, soon they would be
together again.

That was twenty-two years ago. As Eldon strung the tiny string of
lighted lights around the tiny tree his heart couldn't help but think that
time in mortality must be much, much longer than time in eternity. Oh
how he missed his friend, how he missed his partner, how he missed his
precious wife.

Eldon looked into the little cardboard box and pulled out the other
ornaments of memory and hung them from the branches of the tree. Each
one represented a portion of his life. They represented who he was. Each
one came with a memory, a face, a place, or a time. None were frivolous,
all were significant to him and most likely would be impressive to who
ever knew what they stood for.

But as time marches on it leaves in its wake human existence. How many lives have lived on planet earth? How many deeds of valor have been done? How many lives have been saved? How many kind and thought-ful deeds have been done? How many times have the feeble knees been strengthened, and the hanging heads been lifted? The sands of time have covered all but a few, and of those few, who cares?

So it was with Eldon, a life so rich and full, now obscure and forgot-ten. In his kitchen he had himself and his memories to keep each other company. It was now Christmas Eve of his eighty seventh-year. His deco-rations were all now hanging on the tree illuminated by the lights on the tree. Eldon sat on the wooden chair next to the table. He set his bible on the table below the tree and opened the holy writ to Luke chapter one. "And in those days there went out a decree . . ."

Eldon read the words out loud to himself. Every word bringing back the spirit of Christmas past when family and friends gathered around a large freshly cut pine tree and sang the songs of yuletide cheer and where everyone surrounded a large round table covered with the feasts of the season and where love, laughter, and life filled the air.

Eldon closed his eyes and dreamed. In the depth of his dream he heard a knocking on a distant door. It was faint and soft, but seemed to be steady. As if coming from a land far beyond, Eldon could now hear the knocking and it was coming from the door just across from the tiny living room. Arousing his faculties Eldon arose from his wooden seat and walked slowly across the wooden floor and opened the door.

Standing in the doorway was a small boy with a gift-wrapped box in his hand. He had a cap covering his curly brown hair, a warm jacket, and knitted mittens on his hands on which sat the gift. Behind him was his mother, a friendly looking woman with a thick wool coat and a scarf with a knitted hat covering her long black hair. Eldon greeted the lad and the woman and asked how they were this fine Christmas Eve? Ryan, the little ten-year-old boy replied, that they were fine and that it was a wonderful Christmas Eve.

Ryan stretched forth his hand holding the gift-wrapped box toward Eldon. Eldon had no idea what this meant, and without a word took the

box from the hands of the little boy and just looked at the present. He then looked down at him and thanked him for the gift. Ryan just smiled and then after a moment asked, "Are you going to open it?" After a gentle reprimand from his mother, Eldon smiled back at the cheerful boy, and replied, "I will, just as soon as you and your mother come in and have a warm cup of hot chocolate."

Eldon brought in a stool from the main room and sat down on it as Ryan and his mother sat on the two twin wooden chairs in front of the homely appearing Christmas tree. After their cups were filled with warm chocolate and a couple of marshmallows the mother explained how they lived in the same apartment building and had seen Eldon come and go from time to time. They felt bad that they had never taken the time to introduce themselves to him.

They felt that Christmas was just too important of a time for anyone to be alone and so they decided to drop off a gift. Eldon felt a warm feeling permeate the room. He felt a gratitude for the kindness of two other human souls. Surely all mankind are brothers and sisters if we would only let ourselves be.

They asked Eldon about the unusual ornaments hanging from his tree. As Eldon softly touched each ornament and explained it's meaning, they could see a glow surround his eyes, they could feel the passion in his voice. The stories stirred their souls, they cried, they laughed, they felt joy, and they felt sorrow. In the feeling and experiencing and sharing, another Christmas was filled with meaning and purpose.

The hours passed and a friendship was formed, a lonely old man found someone who cared, and a widow and her fatherless son found a grandfatherly figure who had acres of love yet to give.

And so it is with Christmas, it is a time to share, a time to give of ourselves, a time to remember lives lived, a time to remember the child born in a manger in a far away land who can still save us all.

The Lesson

"Mr. Millington," said Sara Benning, poking her head through the door, "I am going to go home now, is there anything you need before I go?" "No," responded Jeff, "Have a wonderful Christmas holiday, and give your little boy my best."

Jeff spun his chair around and stared at the lights of Manhattan perched up on the 43rd floor of his office building. His floor to ceiling picture windows made up three of his four walls. His office, which was as large as most people's apartments, was furnished with elegant yet simple furniture. Limited edition prints adorned the walls, sculptures the end tables, and antique books graced the shelves of his grand bookcase.

He had worked hard to get were he was. The many years of toil, the long hours, the killer business instinct, paid off. He was the emperor of his small kingdom. He had foreseen the impact semi conductors would have and poised himself at the right time. Not a bad showing for a poor ragged boy from Montana. But as he stared out the window watching the myriad of lights racing around in the darkness, his feelings and thoughts were not of how successful he felt, but of the price his success had cost him. Jeff leaned his head back against the leather seat, closing his eyes he let the chair tip gently back allowing the lights of the night to penetrate through the window and dance across his tired face.

"Everything has a price," Jeff said quietly to himself, not noticing a tear roll down his cheek moistening his collar. "And everything has a cost."

"With all my heart," whispered the sweet and gentle voice quivering with emotion. Jeff slid the plain gold ring onto the soft, delicate finger of Lynette. "It isn't much," Jeff said, "but I will always do everything I can to make you happy." "You, make me happy," Lynette replied, quietly emphasizing the word you. "I just want to be with you forever."

It was the most incredible words Jeff thought he would ever hear. Lynette was his best friend since she moved into his neighborhood when they were in the second grade. He had admired her ever since. He had always treated her with the utmost respect even when the other boys teased him and were convinced she had cooties. But Jeff hoped he would catch the disease, if it meant Lynette would take care of him.

There was no happier time in his life than when he knelt down across from her at the altar of marriage gazing into her dark, beautiful eyes. It was the culmination of many years of anticipation, with all the hope, and the fear. He felt as if nothing could ever steal away the incredible joy he felt at that moment.

The joy multiplied four more times. With each new addition to their family, Jeff found himself working harder to provide the necessities for them. He worked extra jobs in the evenings and on weekends. He volunteered for extra hours. It was not long before Jeff was able to save a small amount of money.

He remembered well the day Alvin, his work associate, approached him with an opportunity to "make it big." Although Alvin probably did not realize what he had discovered, Jeff's business sense told him it was big. He took his small savings and leveraged it to acquire a small insignificant semi conductor manufacturer who was in financial difficulties due to poor management. Jeff and Alvin turned the fledgling, struggling company around. The technology, which they possessed, catapulted them into the industry with a vengeance that never slowed down. Jeff eventually bought out Alvin's share when Alvin went into debt foolishly. From there, he was able to increase his manufacturing facilities, develop cutting edge technology, buy out competitors, and increase his holdings. It was amazing, he used to think, how financial success keeps multiplying once you have penetrated a certain threshold. It was as if you could not fail.

Jeff leaned his big leather chair forward and stood up. He walked over to his window and gazed down on the little human figures scurrying around on Wall Street. As Jeff pressed his forehead against the cold windowpane, he wondered what their lives were like.

Where were they coming from? Where were they going? Was it home, to a quiet, silent apartment? Maybe to their families' house with all their brothers and sisters around to celebrate the holidays? What kind of sufferings were they struggling with? What were their joys, their pains, what was their story?

Each little figure dashing around was a person with a name. They were born somewhere. They had a Mother who brought them into the world. Why was he where he was, and they were there where they were?

Rolling around on the glass window Jeff turned to look at his office. His eyes rolled past each object in the room. This was the result of his choices. He made a decision somewhere, someplace, sometime, that this would be his road. "What road did I take that led me here," Jeff whispered, sullenly to himself.

He felt as if the road he had taken had suddenly thickened with a heavy fog, which aided him in losing his way, a fog that lasted through many roads and many turns. It was only recently that the dense fog seemed to dissipate. And with this clearing, Jeff finally saw the tragedy the road he had chosen led him to.

"Oh, Lynette," Jeff cried, bursting out in a flood of tears. He crumpled to the floor. All the emotions and consequences of his foolish choices over the past years engorged through his soul. It was the first time he had allowed the realization of what he had thrown away to take root in his heart. How had he let the most important things in his life vanish? Why could he not feel through the fog and reach for the voice that called to him through tears in the middle of many lonely nights.

As Jeff wept, he felt the bitter sorrow of a soul who had lost a pearl of great price. He remembered well the morning he read the note. He had come home late the night before and never noticed that the beds were empty. Not even when he ate his breakfast by himself in the early hours of the morning did he notice the stillness of a house that had no occupants. Not even when he noticed the note taped to the door handle did he understand what had happened. He remembered reading the note and feeling anger at the unappreciativeness of his ungrateful family. Didn't they realize how hard he had worked for them! All the hours, the effort, the skill, he invested in doing his job as the provider.

He crumpled the note in his hand and tossed it aside as he sternly moved along the winding sidewalk to his car. He rehearsed in his mind what he would expound to his family when he got home. So sure was he that they would be there after this silly notion had passed.

They were not there. Sadly, they never returned.

The many hours he had spent away "providing" for his family increased the distance between him and the ones he had loved. Each minute was a mile; each hour was a hundred, until their roads where at two different ends of the world.

The years had passed, the feelings hardened, until climbing the ladder of success was the only thing of importance. He had not realized the road he had chosen led directly through the fields of loneliness. The exquisite price he had paid in losing his family flooded over him as he sobbed in a heap upon the floor with the lights of success illuminating the 43rd floor.

December 24th, five years to the day, his once cherished Lynette, had sent him her wedding notice announcing her marriage to a Mr. John Harper, of Kalispell, Montana, a bitter Christmas gift. The finality of the notice hardened his heart even more and increased the distance between him and his children. Deep down Jeff realized John was the man he could have been had he chosen the alternate path when the decision was placed before him. John was a simple man, a carpenter by trade. Yet he was happy. He radiated a love for life.

Jeff opened the top left drawer on his desk, pulled out the wedding announcement, and stared at the picture. It was as if a thousand years had passed, another lifetime had come and gone. Yet the pain was as fresh as a sword wound to the heart, which would never heal. "How do I go on," Jeff lamented. "How did I forget about the most precious things I've ever had? How did I lose a priceless gift? How do I survive knowing I will never hold her, ever again? It is too much too endure." he grieved.

He gently placed the wedding announcement on the corner of the desk. He walked to the freestanding designer coat hanger and grabbed his suit coat. He turned out the lights and stared back once more at the culmination of his life. His eyes passed over the different possessions. Each one an equation with lost moments. Turning, he closed the door.

As he approached Sara's desk he pulled two envelopes from his suit pocket and laid them on her desk. One envelope contained a letter to Sarah personally, explaining his decision, with a sizable check, which would take care of her and her son. The second was a letter, a letter of instructions, describing the transfer of all the assets from the corporations to be distributed to the various charities, and turning over the power of attorney to a preselected committee.

Jeff flung his trench coat over his shoulder and opened the outer door of his office that lead into the hallway. Turning back, holding on to the handle of the door, he mentally said good-bye to the road that led him to this dead end. He heard the shutting of the door echo through the empty hall as he faced the elevators that would begin his journey on a different road. A road less traveled.

The Boeing 767 touched down on the tarmac of the airport at Calcutta, India, a country with a million poor. The heat and humidity were intense. A man in khaki pants, tennis shoes, and one bag slung over his shoulder, sweat beading on his forehead, stepped out, and made his way to the airport terminal.

Jeff navigated his way through the crowded airport, dodging his way around passengers, luggage, and livestock. His eyes drank in this new world of people, problems, and hopelessness.

Quietly, Jeff sat in the back seat of the taxi he had secured to take him to the heart of despair. To the very center of the cities impoverished populace, an area with so much misery and utter futility that the word hope had no home. As the taxi bumped along the streets of Calcutta, Jeff watched the view of the city pass by from the car window. The words of a book he had read years before flooded into his mind, [1]"I tell you these things that ye may learn wisdom, that ye may learn, that when ye are in the service of your fellow beings, you are only in the service of your God."

The taxi came to a halt in front of a run down building bearing the sign, "Calcutta's Mission of Hope." Paying the driver what would have amounted to a month's worth of work for him, Jeff stepped out of the taxi and over the cutter which flowed with a black, odorous water and walked up to the door.

He paused a moment to wipe the sweat from his brow which accumulated from the stifling heat and the lack of air conditioning in the taxi. He turned the handle of the old wooden door to the mission. The squeaking of the hinges announced his arrival.

Pushing the door the rest of the way open, Jeff watched the rays of light penetrate the air born dust in a clean but worn out room. The light exposed the sight of Sister Marguerite, a sturdy, weather worn woman, with a face creased with lines that reflected kindness and compassion. She was handing a basket of food and blankets to a little dark haired girl in tattered clothes.

As this little soul scurried past Jeff, she glanced up at him with a smile so rich and deep that he could not help feeling an angel had brushed by him. The exchange of glances with the little girl had been so profound that Jeff found himself passing that brief moment as if it had taken a hundred years. "Her name is Anna," came a sturdy voice.

"Her parents came from a tiny village north of here in order to find a better life in the city. All they found was more hardship and a city with thousands just like them and thousands more who didn't care." Jeff looked up at the voice. "They ended up living in a blanket shelter while her father tried to find work. Unfortunately, in the meantime her mother passed away giving birth as did the infant and several months after that the father died of dysentery leaving only Anna and her little brother Sam."

"I'm Sister Marguerite," the woman continued, as she walked over to Jeff shaking his hand. Sister Marguerite was the nun in charge of the mission. She had been in Calcutta for twelve years helping the poor wretched souls ease their burden of daily life. She had seen the depths of sorrow and despair whose pit was so deep none ever climbed out.

Jeff met the eyes of Sister Marguerite as she introduced herself. Her face showed the lines of hardship, which was like a road map of the years she had served in this den of despair. Yet her eyes had a depth to them that reflected compassion and gentleness in easing the burdens of another of God's children.

Jeff was here to help the mission raise funds to acquire the much-needed supplies they required. He was going to help organize their efforts and help them use their resources to the fullest extent possible. He was going to draw on the years of experience he had gained in the business world and use it to serve someone else, and this time for free.

Jeff went to work. In a short three-month period he had tripled their funds and was able to organize the mission to the point of helping more people with greater aid.

In all this time he had watched little Anna come and go. Every week she would stop by the mission and pick up a large basketful of food, blankets, medicine, and other sundry items. She would carefully pack her basket as to fit as much in it as possible, and then sling the heavy bundle upon her back and leave.

Each time she came, she would smile. Never did she utter an unkind word or bemoan her circumstances. She always spoke of the people who lived on the streets in her section of town. She spoke of Ruhan Mesmir and how he was hoping to find work as a bricklayer any day now and move his family into a small apartment, of Sengala the little old grandmother who was waiting for her grandson to earn enough money to send for her to come to Delhi. Of Sam Naghem, whose father was hoping soon to be able to buy him a wheel chair so he would not have to crawl in the filthy streets. And of Sara, her little friend, who was hoping to get a pair of glasses so her world would not be a blur passing by. Many more tales of sorrow awaiting deliverance from misery would she talk about.

Jeff had spoken with Sister Marguerite numerous times about finding a place for Anna and her brother to live where they would be out of the elements. Each time the Sister had spoken with Anna, she would refuse every offer of a place to stay. She insisted upon staying where she was.

"It is very important," she would say, in her quiet little English with an Indian accent.

Jeff would struggle emotionally each time she would come to load up the supplies offered by the mission and carry the enormous load on such tiny little shoulders. Each time she would refuse his offer to help her carry the basket to her shelter. Jeff had some comfort that at least she was receiving a goodly amount of supplies each week. At least she had enough food, clothing, and blankets to keep her warm and filled.

As the weeks turned into months, Jeff experienced the love that comes from serving others. Not just making sure everything was fiscally in order but of being involved personally. He had given vaccines to children, delivered a baby in a muddy shack with rain pouring in, and held the hand of a frail old man as he passed from this life into a world of rest. He carried a fever stricken mother from the refuse mounds of the city to her dirt floor home and gently laid her on a straw pallet. He had bandaged the wounds of so many little children he became an expert. He had delivered food, hugged dirty faces of little children, and learned to not only wipe the tears from saddened eyes, but to shed tears with them.

He had learned that to serve means to lose oneself in the work, that you must feel and touch the very souls of the people. He understood that love is what will lighten their burdens. There is not enough money in the world to buy every person out of despair. However, there was enough love.

Jeff began to be concerned when he saw Anna. She seemed to be losing weight. She struggled a little more than usual trying to heft her heavy basket upon her shoulders. He asked her if she was feeling all right. She responded as she did every time, that she never felt better.

However, this time Jeff was scared. Her little face had a gray pale look to it, her lips where whiter than usual. She stumbled hefting her basket. He insisted that she stay there. He was going to take her to a doctor.

After she gained her strength, Jeff had arranged for her and her brother to go to America with him. He had fulfilled his personal commitment to the mission and now felt it was his responsibility to take care of these two forgotten children.

Anna pleaded with him to let her go back to her street just once more. Her dark little eyes building up with tears. I must go back, just once more. Jeff's heart struggled with her pleading voice. He would let her return but this time he would carry the load. Just as they were about to leave, a call came in for him. It was the immigration department. Jeff bent down and took Anna by the hand, "Wait right here, I need to take this very important call, I won't be but a minute, I will be right back." Jeff turned and went to the back room, which had served as his makeshift office.

As he hung up the phone, a sigh of relief crossed his lips. Everything had been approved. Little Anna and her brother Sam would be coming to his home in America. Everything had worked out perfectly. He walked out of the room to find the spot where Anna was standing empty. He ran to the door and opened it up. Looking up the street and down the street, he could not see her. It had started to rain. He turned and grabbing his raincoat ran into the street. He knew from the conversations with Anna approximately the area of town she had been living.

It had taken him longer than he had hoped to find where she had gone. As he was crossing the street he stopped and stood in the middle of it with the rain pouring down and looked toward the end of the street. Through the rows of blanket houses lining the street, there towards the end of the street, was Anna with her heavy load.

He watched her for a moment transfixed on what she was doing. Anna would go to each blanket shelter and fold back the flap. She would bend over giving a piece of the goods in her basket to an outstretched hand. She did this to every blanket shelter until her basket was empty, food, and all.

As she left the last shelter, Anna turned and started to walk back down the street to where Jeff was standing. With a sudden flash of understanding Jeff realized what Anna had been doing. Each time she had come to the shelter to load up her basket with food, clothing, and other items, she would take them to these people on the streets of this blanket community, to the poor souls who had been her neighbors. Anna would distribute all of the supplies to them. That was why she was losing weight and looked sickly. She had given all of her food. She had malnourished herself to help those who she felt needed it more than she.

As Anna was walking toward him, Jeff saw her falter a step. He ran up the street as fast as he could to where she was walking. As he reached her, Anna's basket fell from her hands. The world around Jeff seemed to come to a halt. He could not hear the noise of the rain or the sounds of the city. Everything seemed to move in slow motion. All he could see was the droplets of rain running down Anna's face. She was standing silent and motionless in the middle of the street. He could see her eyes gently close and her body begin to slowly fall over. He stretched out his arms just in time to catch her little body before it touched the ground.

He sat there in the muddy street, rain dancing on the ground around him, with Anna lying in his arms. Her breathless body had a glow about it. Her face was graced with a smile as the rain washed off the dirt. She was gone. A pair of glasses still clenched in her little hand. She had lost her life giving of herself. The tears fell from Jeff's eyes and mixed with the rains of Calcutta as they ran down Anna's lifeless face. He gently rocked her back and forth pressing his lips upon her forehead.

After what seemed like an eternity Jeff gently lifted the little girl cradling her in his arms and slowly walked back to the mission. Sorrow never seemed so heavy.

"Would you like something to drink," came a soft voice, as if from a hundred miles away. Jeff opened his eyes and quietly said, "No thanks," to the flight attendant standing over his seat. She could see that his eyes were moist. "Are you alright," she asked, as she gently touched his arm. "No," he replied, "but I will be." "Is there anything I can do?" "Nothing that an angel hasn't done already."

The flight attendant wished him a Merry Christmas on this the twenty-fourth of December. It was one year to the day since he had left his office of money and business on the forty-third floor of Manhattan. It seemed another lifetime ago. This twenty-fourth found him with a Christmas gift that was priceless.

He turned to look at Sam, Anna's brother, asleep in the seat next to him. He held his arm and then rested his head on the back of the seat. He knew everything would be okay. He had lost his family on Wall Street, but had found hope on the streets of Calcutta. Yes, he would be all right. He had once again found the path he had lost so many years ago in the fog.

[1]Mosiah 3:16 The Book of Mormon Another Testament of Jesus Christ

159

Merry Christmas!

Made in the USA
Lexington, KY
30 November 2019